The Marriage Meltdown
Maggie Linn Sharpe

Paperback Edition ISBN-13: 979-8-9923370-6-8

eBook Edition ISBN-13: 979-8-9923370-5-1

Cover design by Maggie Linn Sharpe.

Edited by: Lily Luchesi, Partners In Crime Book Services

Also by Maggie

Author's Note

THE MARRIAGE MELTDOWN INCLUDES one of the more polarizing tropes out there in the romance world so I thought I'd include a note about it here.

I'm of the opinion that the "surprise baby" trope should only be a surprise to the character and never to the reader. I know it can be a sensitive subject so all trope lists, blurbs, character art, and summaries have included the mention that Jessie will be experiencing an unexpected pregnancy in this book.

Jessie's pregnancy and birth experience (off page) are mostly uncomplicated and while her pregnancy is unexpected and comes at an inconvenient time, it is a wanted pregnancy by both parents once they get over the shock.

If a pregnant main character isn't your cup of tea, that's completely fine. Feel free to rejoin us for Cass and Griffin's story in The Chemistry Complication. All of my books can be read as standalones, so you can pick up with book four.

Never be afraid to protect your heart and your mental health!

xo, Maggie

To anyone living with less than they deserve.

I hope you find the courage to demand change or walk away from anything

no longer serving you.

Contents

From the Anniversary Journal of: Dan & Jessie Chase

Wedding Memories

Hers:

Dan and I are finally married!!! My mother-in-law (ahh! How fun is it that I can call Marlene that now?) gave us this super cute journal to document each year of our marriage. Dan thinks it's silly, but I think it will be so fun to look back at these memories when we're old and gray.

Our wedding was small (but still <u>beautiful</u>, don't get me wrong) since our budget was pretty much nonexistent. Just a few of our friends and family at the courthouse, and then we had a reception party in Leena's gram's backyard. Leena and Annie helped me decorate it, and the yard looked like a fairytale.

I was bummed Mom and Dad didn't come. I guess they're still mad I wouldn't move home and go to grad school like they wanted me to, but hopefully they'll come around when they see how happy and successful Dan and I are going to be. Yes, we're young and he's still proving himself in the minors, but I know without a doubt, Dan Chase and I are forever. I refuse to go any longer without being by his side. Our life together is going to be perfect!

I already have a job lined up with an event planner in Pennsylvania. Leena and Annie are going to help me get moved in since Dan has a string of away games next week. When he's back, I'll have turned his bachelor pad apartment into our first home together. I love him so much, and I'm so ready to be the best wife I can be.

I guess that's it for now! See you in a year!

XO, Jessie

His:

Jessie's making me write in this stupid thing. I think it's dumb, but I love my wife, so here we are. The wedding was good. I don't really care about these kinds of things, and I would have been fine with just the courthouse part, but Jessie really wanted the party afterwards. I was glad Mom could come up from Charlotte for it. She would have been sad to miss it.

I wish we were going on a honeymoon, but I had barely enough time off with the All-Star Break to make the wedding work, and then I'll be back on the road. Maybe in the off-season we'll be able to scrape together enough cash to go on a vacation. At least when I'm done with this road trip, Jessie will be there waiting for me. I'm sure she'll be rearranging and decorating to her heart's content while I'm gone.

I'M GONNA PROVE TO HER PARENTS THAT I CAN TAKE CARE OF HER. I'LL BE CALLED UP TO THE MAJORS ANY TIME NOW. I CAN FEEL IT. I'LL DO EVERY-THING IN MY POWER TO PROVIDE FOR JESS AND ANY KIDS WHO COME ALONG. I'M GONNA SHOW THEM. WE'LL BE LIVING THE GOOD LIFE, AND EVERYTHING WILL BE PERFECT.

—DAN

Chapter One

Jessie

Almost 10 Years Later

THE HARSH FEBRUARY WIND bites at the back of my neck as I grab my load of shopping bags out of the back of my SUV. I'm able to gather them all in one trip, my hands full as I hurry to hit the garage door button with my elbow, closing out the frigid air.

I hustle inside the warm house and walk into our beautiful open-concept kitchen. Dropping the pile of bags on the huge marble island and sorting through them, putting any food away. I grab the bag with the ovulation test strips and pregnancy tests and take it with me to stash in my bathroom after I show Dan.

The baby-making plan is a go this month. We haven't been actively preventing pregnancy up to this point, and now I'm ready to kick it up a notch and start trying for a baby. I've got all the apps downloaded to track my cycle and a thermometer to take my temperature every day, like the piles of research I found suggested. My type-A planner brain is all over this.

Dan's car was in the garage, so I know he's home, but he's not in the living room or the den I like to refer to as his man cave. Since he retired from baseball in the fall, these are his usual spots for this time of the afternoon. He's still been working out with his buddies from the team regularly, but other than those workouts, he's usually watching sports on the massive

TV or playing video games. He's been making the most of his new, light schedule.

I hear some rustling upstairs, so he must be in our bedroom. I bounce up the stairs, excited to see him, especially with our bed nearby. Maybe I can break out an ovulation strip before we get to it.

Can I take an ovulation test in the middle of the day, or is it supposed to be in the morning? Another fertility question to Google later!

When I enter the room, I immediately take notice of his large suitcase sitting on the bed, almost full. My stomach instantly drops to somewhere around my pink fuzzy winter socks. I hear Dan moving around in the en suite bathroom, but I'm frozen at the sight and sound of his packing.

What the fuck is going on?

"Dan?" I call out in a shaky voice, already filled with dread.

The rustling sounds in the bathroom go silent before he calls back, "Oh, hey, baby. I wasn't sure when you'd be back."

"Are you going somewhere?"

There's a long pause before he exits the bathroom, zipping up his travel toiletry case. My eyes drop to the case as he adds it to the suitcase and zips the whole thing shut. I take a step back and study the man I've loved for nearly my entire adult life.

Dan is just as handsome as the day I met him during my freshman year of college, his senior year, with his almost black hair and his flawless olive skin. His hair is a little more stylish now, cut short on the sides and left messy on top with small traces of gray showing at the temples. Small lines have appeared alongside his eyes, making him look distinguished.

I meet his eyes, and instead of the cocky mischief he wore in his sparkling blue-green eyes back in college, they shine with guilt and apprehension. He tugs nervously at the back of his neck, making his impressive biceps pop, but I can't get distracted by his unfairly hot body because I'm pretty sure I'm not gonna like what he has to say next.

"Coach called. The rookie they were bringing up to replace me got hurt. They want me to come to spring training to fill in. Probably for the whole season."

Before he retired, Dan was the starting catcher for the Flash, the professional baseball team here in Fort Starling, Ohio. His words are like a punch to the stomach. I should have known when he didn't make any formal announcement of his retirement that he'd go back on his decision.

Again.

I don't say anything at first, stunned by the hurt and anger coursing through my veins. I stare at the man in front of me, the one I have loved through the ups and downs of almost ten years of marriage. Through his getting called up to the majors, through being traded multiple times, and through having to move our entire lives to new cities. Through my parents practically disowning me and cutting me off financially for getting married straight out of college at twenty-one. I've loved him through having to rebuild my event planning business from scratch multiple times, and putting having kids on hold. Through his breaking promises and blowing me off over and over again.

I let the fact that he is once again breaking his promise sink in as I search his features. This will be the third time he's gone back on his word about retirement. With even more instances of him deciding the course of our lives without having so much as a conversation with me, I'm not sure I even recognize the man standing in front of me. He should probably be embarrassed that, as a professional baseball player, he's not more worried about what happens after three strikes.

"Jessie Baby, say something."

"What is there to say? You promised. You're breaking your promise. *Again.*" My voice sounds cold, almost robotic. I wish I could say I'm surprised, but part of me expected this to happen. Part of me has been waiting for the other shoe to drop ever since last season ended. I wish I hadn't gotten my hopes up about the idea of a baby, though. The thought makes my chest ache and my stomach flip.

"I meant it when I said I was gonna retire this year. I did. I even told everyone I was done. But... the team needs me."

"And I don't? What about trying for a baby? Are we putting it on hold now? Should I just get right back on the pill now, since you'll be gone again this season?"

"I've said all along it shouldn't matter if I'm still playing for us to have a baby. You're the one who wanted to wait until I retired!" he snaps angrily, reminding me of the fight we've been having continuously over the last several years.

We were finally there. It really seemed like he was going to hold up his end of the bargain this time. He was going to give us the chance to focus on repairing the damage the last ten years have had on our relationship. To build back what every little piece of neglect from him has eroded. I wanted so badly to believe this year would be different. This would be the year he chose me, *chose us*, and our future. But nothing's different. He's leaving, and once again, I didn't have any say in the matter.

"So that's it. No discussion, no warning. You're off to spring training like normal. I'm supposed to go about my day like you didn't just drastically change the next year of my life without so much as a heads up."

Dan scrubs a hand down his face. He had to know this wasn't gonna go over well. He had to have seen this fight coming. I don't know why he's so frustrated; he's the one who just keeps doing whatever the fuck he wants with no consequences.

"I'm sorry, baby. I am, but it's just one more season. I'm doing this for us. One more season can set us up even better for the future."

One more season? I don't believe him. At this point, it's become painfully obvious I can't believe anything he says. Who knows? Maybe he had always planned on playing this year and was just stringing me along. Pinning it on wanting to make us more financially stable is just sad. We have enough in our bank accounts to last us a lifetime after his successful career in the majors and all the endorsements and sponsorships that came with it.

"You know this isn't about money. What about what I need? What if I need you to be done? What if I *need* you to keep your promises?"

"I don't understand why I'm the one who has to give up my dreams here? Baseball has been good to us. I haven't heard you complaining about this big, beautiful house you could decorate however you want. The clothes, the vacations, all of this is possible thanks to baseball. Why do I have to decide between my career and a family?"

I can literally feel my heart breaking in my chest with a dull ache that takes my breath away. He's the one sacrificing his dreams? He's making it painfully obvious that he doesn't see me. He doesn't see the way I had to start over from square one with my business every time he was traded. The way I've waited for him to be an active participant in our life together. And if he doesn't see me, I'm having a hard time finding a reason to stay. The thought threatens to break me in half, but I don't let any of it show on my face. It won't do any good.

He zips the suitcase and wheels it to the bedroom door before coming back to gather me in his arms. I let myself melt into him just for a moment. It might be the last time, even though he doesn't know it yet. He's expecting me to let it go. To forgive him again and go back to being the perfect baseball wife. I don't think I have it in me.

"I'm sorry, Jess. But I have to go; my ride's here." He gives me a perfunctory kiss on the lips, barely a peck, before grabbing his suitcase and taking off down the hallway. "Love you, baby!" he calls as he leaves, an afterthought on his way back to the game he can't do without.

Through the big window at the front of our room, I watch as he gets in a town car and drives away into the frozen February day. I stay still, staring out the window for several minutes before shaking myself from the trance his departure put me in.

I want to be furious. I want to scream and wail and throw things. I'll probably get there, but for now, I'm numb.

I spend the evening wandering the rooms of this big, beautiful house he so casually threw in my face. My dream house. What was supposed to be our forever home. Now I'm here alone. *Again.* Knowing deep down, I'll be saying goodbye soon.

When he texts to let me know he made it to Arizona safely, I don't respond. And when he calls that night for one of our daily check-ins, a staple of our marriage until now, any time he's been away, I ignore the call. I'll talk to him when I'm ready. When my next move is figured out. Because one thing is sure, I can't go back to the way it's always been.

I'm done.

From the Anniversary Journal of: Dan & Jessie Chase

Year One

Hers:

What a whirlwind of a first year! Dan was called up to the majors this season (YAY!!!), so we moved from Pennsylvania to Indiana. The schedule is a bit crazier and more intense; he's definitely not home as much, and when he is, he seems stressed, but he's living his dream! I'm so proud of him!!

We're a little farther from Fort Starling this time, but I've still been able to visit Leena and Annie a couple of times. The other wives and girlfriends are friendly enough, so I haven't been too lonely while Dan's on the road.

I found another event planner to work for here once we moved. I really do love working events. I love seeing the vision come together; turning an empty ballroom into something beautiful is its own special magic. Eventually, I'd love to own my own business, but I'm happy to learn from Michelle for now! Dan said something about me not needing to work, but what on earth would I do with my time while he's gone so much? Plus, I like having money that's just mine. Not my husband's, not my parents', mine.

Speaking of parents, Mom and Dad still haven't forgiven me for going against their wishes and getting married, so I don't hear from them much. Even with Dan getting called up, they're still pissed I didn't follow their exact plan for me. They wanted me to become a cookie-cutter version of them. Going to grad school, getting a corporate job, and marrying someone they deemed worthy were all designed for me to step into their life. A life I never wanted. They like to pretend they were looking out for me, but they really wanted control. We'll show them we don't need them. They can keep their money and their fake support.

I love having a home of our own, and it was fun getting to decorate with a much bigger budget than I had last time around. I wish Dan would give me a bit more input. It is our home after all, but he said he didn't care what things looked like as long as I was happy. It's sweet, even though it was a bit frustrating.

Dan is on the road a lot, of course, but we still get so much more time together than we did while we were long-distance, so it's fine. We make the most of the time we have, if you know what I mean!

I can't believe we've been married for a whole year now! One year down, forever to go!

See you next year!

XO, Jessie

His:

Jessie still! I don't think Dan's gonna write in this thing. I asked him to, but he said he didn't have time. Oh well! This journal can just be for me to look back on our memories! Maybe I'll use it to vent about the silly things I get frustrated with Dan about, and then it'll be funny to read my whining when we're old and gray!

Chapter Two
Dan

"WHAT THE FUCK ARE you doing here, man?" Bailey's voice cuts through the open-concept living room of our shared condo as I enter through the front door. I got lucky he didn't line up a new roommate for this year, opting to have the two-bedroom condo we usually share to himself for spring training.

I had hoped he wouldn't mind my taking my same room again this year, but he sounds pissed to see me. Bailey Turner, the Flash pitcher and one of my best friends, stands in the kitchen mixing a protein shake, and he looks as angry as he sounds. His dark brown eyes are narrowed at me in accusation, arms crossed, waiting for my reply.

"Coach called. The rookie catcher they brought up got hurt last week, and they wanted me here to fill in." I shrug like it's no big deal that I'm here, and his eyes narrow even more.

"You shouldn't fucking be here, Dan. What are you doing?" he says sharply.

"I told you. The team needs me."

"And Jessie? What did she have to say about it?" He plants his hands on his hips and glares at me, knowing exactly how Jessie was bound to feel about my not retiring when I said I would.

I cringe as I think about the look on her face when I told her I was headed back to spring training. I expected her to be furious with me. I deserve it for breaking my promise again. But she was eerily calm this time. She didn't scream or cry. She just wore a look of betrayal that shredded my heart into little pieces. The defeated slump of her shoulders is going to haunt me for a while. I'm gonna have to grovel hard to get back on her good side this time.

I don't know why she can't see that I'm doing this for us. I don't know what kind of work I'll be able to do after baseball is done. Shouldn't I cash in for as long as I can to set us up for our future? I know we have plenty in the bank now, but each year I keep playing pads our accounts for the future. I watched my mom struggle and scrimp to make ends meet. I refuse to put Jessie in that same position.

"She was upset, but we'll work through it. It's just one more season."

Bailey studies me with his brows furrowed. He knows I've been promising Jessie I'll retire, and I'm sure he's thinking about what his fiancée, who happens to be one of Jessie's best friends, would say to all of this. I can almost guarantee Leena will rip me a new one if she gets the chance.

"I thought you guys were gonna start trying for a kid?" he finally asks.

Guilt stabs me again, making my stomach clench. I'm such a hypocrite when it comes to the baby shit. I've been pushing for years for us to start our family, but when Jessie went off the pill a couple of months ago and it became a real option, I realized how little I know about being a dad. I didn't have a dad in my life, so how am I supposed to know how to be one? My mom raised me entirely on her own, and my dad was never in the picture. All the freaking out about the possibility of fatherhood made Coach's offer that much more enticing.

"We still can. She's the one being stubborn about waiting for me to retire." I shrug again, hoping he'll drop this conversation already.

Bailey's silent for a long moment. He stares me down with a deep frown on his face and pulls his hand through his dark brown hair as he studies me. I was hoping for a friendlier reception when I rolled up to our condo, but I get he's looking out for me. And for Jessie.

"I think you're making a mistake," he says quietly but firmly. His tone is ominous, and so full of sincerity, it makes my heart clench. I swallow hard. I have to believe he's exaggerating. Blowing things out of proportion.

"It'll be fine. I'm already here, and it's gonna be a good final season." I say casually. If I say it enough times, maybe it will become true.

"If you say so. But I'll tell you this. Leena is my entire world. If I have to pick sides because you made bad choices, I'm gonna be Team Jessie. I love you, man, but I love Leena more."

I bark out a laugh, grateful for him breaking the tension. "That's fair, man, but it's not gonna come to that. Jessie's pissed now, but she'll get over it."

Bailey shakes his head disbelievingly. "I hope you're right."

I hope I'm right too.

I pat Bailey on the shoulder and drag my suitcase up the stairs to get unpacked and ready for training in the morning. This year we kept the lease on the same condo for the whole year, so my familiar furniture is already set up how I like it in my room.

The king-sized bed is in the corner with a small nightstand next to it. A long dresser sits against the wall alongside the bed, a large TV sitting in the center. A soft navy blue rug covers the floor. Jessie's contribution to the room last year. I just have to make up the bed and put all my stuff away.

I try calling Jessie as I settle into bed, but she doesn't answer. She didn't respond to the text I sent when my plane landed, either, leaving my message on read. I try not to let her silence bother me. It makes sense that she still needs to cool off. I'm sure we'll talk tomorrow.

It'll be fine, I tell myself over and over as I try to fall asleep. Even in my head, it doesn't quite sound true, but I keep repeating it, anyway.

Everything will be fine.

Everything is not fine. It's been over two weeks since I've heard my wife's voice. Two fucking weeks since I've seen her beautiful face, and I'm going crazy. Even when I was first drafted, and Jessie was still in school, we didn't go this long without talking or FaceTiming. At a minimum, we would send texts throughout the day.

I've tried calling her every day, sometimes multiple times a day. I've sent countless texts, but she hasn't responded to a single one. I'm starting to freak out here. What if something happened to her? A jolt of guilt hits me for leaving her all alone in that big house, and I'm seeing the wisdom of her holding off on getting pregnant while I'm away so much.

This morning, I finally got desperate and begged her in a text to talk to me.

Me:

> Baby, please. I'm begging you, literally begging. Please answer my call or call me back. I need to hear your voice. I need to know you're okay. If you don't talk to me, I'm gonna call the cops to check on you.

Jessie:

> Fine. Text me when you're done with your game today, and we can FaceTime.

I'm a little relieved she's still paying attention to the game schedule. She's gotta be close to forgiving me if she's keeping such close tabs on what I'm doing. She probably needed to look it up so she could help plan WAG Weekend, the weekend when a bunch of the wives, girlfriends, and partners come to visit. It's a Flash tradition. We all pretend they're surprising us, and it's a ton of fun. They come to a spring preseason game, and we all go out after.

WAG Weekend is always so good for us. I can't wait. It'll be the perfect weekend to make it up to her that I put off retiring again. I shoot her a text back to confirm I'll text her when the game's over.

Me:

> I will, Jessie Baby. I love you.

She doesn't respond, and it makes my stomach roll with unease. Is she still so pissed she won't say she loves me? I thought her willingness to

FaceTime was a sign she was ready to forgive me. Maybe she's just busy today and didn't get a chance to respond. I wish I knew what events she had on the calendar.

Huh, why haven't I asked her to share her work schedule?

I push her lack of response and my new wave of guilt out of my mind and move on with my warm-ups before our spring game starts. My shoulder hurts today, and I probably shouldn't even be playing. Honestly, I should probably be retiring, like I told my wife I was. The unsettled feeling from before prickles under my skin again, and I shake my head hard to get rid of it.

"Chase, you good?" Coach calls out, eyeing me warily. He called me personally, asking me to be here instead of going through my agent, but I can tell he's concerned about the state of my shoulder.

"All good, Coach," I lie.

He studies me for a moment before shaking his head and walking back to the dugout. I pull my catcher's mask on to hide from any further scrutiny.

The game gets underway, and it's clear to everyone in the ballpark, my head isn't in it. I fumble to grab a bunted hit, my throws to teammates are off, and I strike out all three times I am   up to bat. By the time I hit the showers, I'm sore and pissed off. I've got to get my head on straight and fast, or this season is going to be a shitshow.

I'm anxious to get Jessie on the phone, so I race back to the condo and shoot off a text letting her know I'm home. I'm so ready to see her face and put the last couple of weeks of silent anger behind us. I get myself settled into my bed with an icepack for my shoulder, just as Jessie's FaceTime comes through.

Time to get things back on track.

Chapter Three

Jessie

I'VE SPENT THE LAST couple of weeks since Dan left packing up some of what I want to take with me from our house. I'll have to do a more thorough round of packing once I decide where I'm going long-term, but for now, I have the things I'm hoping to move over to the apartment above the Songbird Café and Bar. Leena, one of my best friends, owns the café, and I know the apartment is empty now that our other best friend, Annie, has moved out.

I haven't told Dan yet. In fact, I haven't been speaking to him at all. I won't be here when he comes back from spring training. I'm done. There's nothing left in me to give to this marriage, and I can't stay here alone any longer. I have to get out of here before I drive myself crazy.

I've been avoiding his calls and ignoring texts, so he has to know something's coming. Normally, we talk every day while he's away, but I haven't been ready to confront him yet. Even last year, when I was furious he broke his promise to retire, I still talked to him every day of training camp and visited him during WAG Weekend with the other wives and girlfriends. Hell, I planned the whole thing like I always do. Of course, we fought while I was there, putting a damper on what is usually a fun weekend.

Today's the day, though. He sent me a pleading text message this morning, begging me to call him so we could talk. They had an earlier game today, so he'll be back at his condo soon. I told him to let me know when he's done, and he agreed. It's time to tell him our almost ten years of marriage are done. I feel shitty for doing it over the phone, but I can't wait for him to come back, and I'm sure as shit not flying out to Arizona just to end things.

It's good timing since I'm headed over to the Songbird for a girls' night tonight. I'll need Leena and Annie after I have this conversation. I promised to help Annie pack up her stuff from the apartment over the bar since she just moved in with her hunky physical therapist boyfriend. I'm pretty sure Leena will be cool with my moving into the apartment space until I get back on my feet.

My phone dings with a text, and my heart stops for a moment, and my stomach bottoms out. I clench my eyes shut as my heart races. *Shit. Am I going to be sick?* Looking down at my phone, I see a message from Dan letting me know he's back at his condo and ready for me to call anytime. I take a few deep breaths to slow my racing pulse, mentally preparing myself for the worst conversation of my life. It's now or never.

I hit the video button, and the FaceTime tone echoes through the living room of our big, lonely house before his handsome face appears. His tan has gotten deeper thanks to the Arizona sun, and he's propped shirtless in bed, an ice pack wrapped around his bad shoulder. His face breaks into a dazzling smile.

I don't return it. I can see myself on the phone screen, and honestly, I look pretty rough. My long blond hair is pulled into a messy bun, my pale face is drawn, and my usually bright blue eyes look dull. Dan doesn't seem to notice.

"Jessie Baby! It's so fucking good to see your face." He sounds so relieved I've finally called him. A wave of guilt floods me, knowing I'm about to break his heart. Even though it's his own fault, it hurts me to hurt him.

"Hey." I swallow hard, trying to get the words to come. "How are you?"

He frowns, sensing my weird tone. "I'm okay. Shoulder's pretty tight, but I'm working through it. I played like shit today, so I'll need to step up my game as the season gets going." He's chatting away as if everything is completely normal between us. Like he didn't shatter my heart with his latest broken promise. He finally seems to realize I haven't responded and studies my face. He swallows and takes a breath. "Is everything alright, baby?"

Is he really asking? Like, I haven't been completely freezing him out for the last couple of weeks?

"Dan..." My voice cracks, but I swallow and continue. "I can't do this anymore."

"Ah, baby, I know the distance sucks. You could always come hang out here for training. I...I'm not sure what events you have on your schedule." He tugs at the back of his neck. He's never paid any attention to my event schedule. The only time he cared was when it conflicted with a game day. "We could—"

"Dan, I'm not talking about the distance. I'm talking about us. I can't do it anymore."

Dan goes still on the screen, brow furrowed. "I don't understand. What can't you do?"

"Us. Our marriage. It's...it's over." Tears have started to flow down my face, but I don't wipe them away.

"Jessie Baby. I know another season isn't what you wanted, but it's not a reason to give up on us." His tone is placating. Condescending. It snaps something inside of me, and I'm less concerned about hurting him than I was before.

I let out a humorless laugh. "What about years of broken promises? What about you implying I've never sacrificed for your dreams? What about you not consulting me on major life decisions over and over?"

Dan's lips straighten into a line, his jaw clenching, fighting the urge to argue with my list of his shortcomings. "Baby. Don't do this over the phone. When I get home, we can sit down and make a plan to work on us."

I scoff again, the anger that's been slowly eating away at me over the years seeping out. "I'm not sure what that would do since I can't trust anything you say." I take a deep breath and blow it out. The tears streaming down my face are making it hard to see my phone screen. I need to be finished with this conversation. "Look. I'm sorry for doing this over the phone, but I can't wait weeks until you're back to be done with this."

"No. We can work this out. Jessie, I love you." His voice turns pleading and desperate. I can't handle much more of this.

"I love you, too, Dan," I sob. I can see tears glistening in his eyes now, and it's breaking what was left of my heart. "But I can't be with you anymore. I'm sorry."

"Jess—"

I end the call without letting him finish. I can't keep listening to him give me every placating promise he can think of. None of it will help because I don't trust his promises anymore. He's shown me over and over, I'm not a priority in his life. I'm not worth the effort. This isn't the life I wanted, and I'm finally doing what's best for me.

My phone lights up with him trying to call me back, but I click the button to ignore the call. I can't keep discussing this with him tonight. It won't lead to anything productive and will only end up hurting us both worse. After the third call, I turn my phone completely off so I don't have to see his name and smiling face on my screen.

I grab my overnight bag and car keys so I can head over to the Songbird. I need to get to my girls now, so I can break down completely. Before I walk out, I take a long look at this beautiful home I love so much. I know I'll be back to get the rest of my things, but it won't be the same.

Everything is different now.

Annie and Leena took the news of my leaving Dan in stride. They seemed surprised by my announcement, which is fair. I've kept a lot of my feelings about my marriage to myself these last few years. They comforted me and confirmed I can move into the apartment here, before sending me down to the bar to get settled in before everything gets going. I have a sneaking suspicion they needed a few minutes to confer on the best way to handle my sobbing meltdown.

I lean my elbows on the bar top and cover my face with my hands, trying to pull myself together before the usual open mic crowd trickles in. The Songbird Café hosts open mic nights twice a week that have become wildly popular. Leena started it when she opened the bar because she likes to sing depressing ballads and always feels like a bummer at karaoke nights. They're always a good time, and I'm hoping to work out some of these emotions on the stage tonight.

Leena is the strongest singer among us, but all three of us have been musical theater   obsessed since we were kids. It's actually one of the things that bonded Leena, Annie, and me when we met in the seventh grade. I told the girls I wanted to sing some Taylor Swift, so that's just what I'm going to do, right after I drown my sorrows in some tequila.

"Here you go, Jess," Cass, the bar manager, says as she sets down a double shot of tequila and a Diet Coke in front of me. Cass studies me with wary eyes. I'm guessing Leena already texted her from upstairs to give her a heads-up about my emotional state. "You okay?"

I blow out a big breath of air. I take the shot quickly and promptly cough and sputter after the tequila burns its way down my throat. Cass's eyebrows shoot up, but she doesn't say anything.

"Ugh, I guess I'm out of practice," I say between coughs, and give her a polite smile. "I'll be fine."

She gives me a small nod and moves a little way down the bar, getting things prepped for the night. I wouldn't consider Cass a close friend; we have different personalities. I tend to come on too strong, talk too much, and she's more reserved and sarcastic. But she's had Leena's back in the couple of years since she opened the bar, and came through for her when

Leena and Bailey were having issues, so we have a grudging respect for each other. We just have nothing in common.

Annie and Leena appear from the back kitchen area and approach me cautiously. They take the barstools on either side of me. Leena picks up my empty shot glass and gives it a sniff. She wrinkles her nose and shoves the glass away from her.

"Ugh, tequila?" She groans.

"It's a tequila shots sort of night," I say, sharper than I intended.

Her expression softens, and she reaches out to squeeze my hand. "Makes sense. But if you think I'm taking tequila shots with you, you're nuts."

I laugh softly. It's well known in our group, Leena won't touch anything with tequila in it, thanks to an infamous bucket of margaritas incident in college. She drank the better part of the bucket by herself and then proceeded to use the bucket when she threw it all back up. Now she can't even smell tequila without getting queasy.

"I know. You can pick whatever liquor you want, but you're not letting me do shots alone." She nods, and we both aim our pointed looks at Annie, who's been keeping quiet on the other side of me. She hates shots, so I'm not surprised she's been trying to avoid notice.

"Do I have to?" Annie whines.

"Yes," Leena and I say in unison.

"Ick, fine. I want something sweet, though. I'm not shooting straight liquor."

Cass comes back over to us, smirking. Leena smiles at her and shakes her head over Annie's antics.

"Let's do a shot of tequila, a shot of gin, and a buttery nipple."

We all laugh at Leena's order, and Annie shrugs   .

"Sounds good to me. If you maniacs are gonna peer pressure me into shots, it better taste good."

Cass chuckles at us and pours out the shots.

"Oh, wait! Cass, do a shot with us!" Leena exclaims before we can drink them.

"Just one," Cass says sternly. She makes eye contact with me and gives me a conspiratorial smile as she pours herself a tequila shot. Maybe we have something in common after all.

Annie, Leena, and I all sputter through the shot while Cass throws it back without even making a face.

"Fuck, Cass, you're such a badass," I sputter out.

She smiles serenely, pours us each another shot, and disappears into the kitchen area to continue her prep work.

"Alright. What Taylor song did you want to sing tonight?" Leena asks as she pulls up the karaoke software on the bar's laptop. "We wanna do some 'Shake it Off'?"

"No. I want 'The Story of Us.' It feels like the right Taylor song for ending a thirteen-year relationship."

I don't miss Leena and Annie sharing a worried glance at my answer, but I focus on my next shot while they have a telepathic conversation over my head.

"Um, so have you actually told Dan you're leaving? Or is this something you just decided?" Annie asks cautiously.

"I told him tonight. I decided it the day he left for spring training."

"Why didn't you call us?" The concern in Leena's voice is palpable.

"I needed to tell Dan first. And I was putting it off a bit. I wanted to make sure I was sure, and I packed up some of the house."

"Oh wow. So this wasn't a heat-of-the-moment decision. You've really thought about this," Annie says in a small voice. Any hopes they had that I was having a dramatic moment are going swiftly out the window, and they're taking the situation seriously now. Leena swallows hard before walking around behind the bar. She wordlessly pours each of us another round, and we all shoot them back in silence.

"Total Eclipse of the Heart" warbled out by a seventy-five-year-old man should be a strange phenomenon, but it's not actually weird for Songbird's open mic. Fred Chambers, grandfather of seven and retired accountant, is belting out the power ballad like his life depends on it. It's pretty standard fare for Fred, who usually performs something wild and flamboyant. In true Fred form, he pairs his performance with a wardrobe straight from an eighties power rocker's closet, right down to the leather pants and eyeliner. My tequila-soaked brain finds it endlessly entertaining.

When Fred is done with his performance, the whole bar cheers and claps for him. He's a favorite with open mic regulars, but he's also been a staple in our lives since we were little. He and his wife, Gail, were good friends with Leena's gram, so they were always around at family and holiday gatherings. It was amazing growing up with an extra set of grandparents floating around, and I never missed a chance to latch onto Leena and Annie's found family.

My family dynamic has always been tense, even before I married Dan against their wishes. Financially, they gave me everything I could ever need and then some. I had expensive clothes, did any activity I wanted, and had my college completely paid for. But my parents weren't around much. I spent more time with nannies, housekeepers, and drivers than I did with them. Now, as an adult, they're not a part of my life other than occasional phone calls where we share a stilted and awkward conversation until one of us makes an excuse to hang up.

I shake my head, clearing the thoughts of my parents, and it makes me slip a bit on my barstool. I grab the bar to steady myself.

"You good, Jess? You look a little wobbly there," Annie says, concern obvious on her face. Annie and Leena both stopped taking shots after the first couple, so I'm the only one feeling tipsy.

"I'm fine." I do my best not to slur my words. I'm not drunk, but I'm not sober either. "I want to sing again, Leens."

"Okay, what do you want to sing?" Leena asks cautiously. I can see her debating whether she should let me back up on the stage.

"I want to do 'Back to Before' from *Ragtime*."

She winces, and I know she's thinking of the devastating lyrics of the song, but it's a perfect "empowered woman moving on from a marriage that's not working" song. Leena studies me for a minute before giving in.

I'm about halfway through the song when I realize I've made a mistake. I am not strong enough, and possibly too drunk, to make it through this song unscathed. The tears start when I sing the line about letting him dream for me. My voice cracks on the word 'wife,' hating the way the past tense of the line sounds. I finish the song in a puddle of tears, unable to get them to stop. I'm a lot drunker than I thought I was.

Leena pulls me off the small stage and wraps her arm around my shoulder. She murmurs something to Cass and leads me toward the front door of the bar.

"Time to go, Jess," she murmurs in my ear. Annie flanks my other side, and I see she has my coat, purse, and overnight bag. We bundle up against the chilly late February night, and I let my two best friends lead me to Leena's car as I continue to cry.

I can't seem to stop the tears now that they've started again, and it's only partially the tequila's fault. I cry the entire way to Leena and Bailey's sprawling house. Even as Leena helps me change into my pajamas and tucks me into her guest bed with an enormous glass of water and ibuprofen, the tears keep coming. They soak my hair and the pillow beneath my head, and they only stop when I finally fall asleep.

Chapter Four
Dan

MY ALARM IS AN unwelcome sound, and I hurry to shut it off. After trying to call Jessie back like a hundred times with no response, I spent the night tossing and turning. Last night had to be a bad dream, right? There's no way my wife of ten years is leaving me, right?

The thought makes me sit up in bed and grab my phone, desperate to check if she called or even texted me back. Anything to give me hope she didn't mean the things she said on the phone last night. I can't believe she's taking this fight so far. I know she's mad, but threatening to leave me is a new low for us.

With no response from my wife, I collapse back onto the bed, a sick feeling taking over my stomach. This is the worst fight we've ever had. No matter how mad Jessie's been in the past, she never stopped responding. The unease in my gut is spreading up my chest, making a lump linger in my throat as I hit her number to try to call her. Straight to voicemail. Again.

Shit. She's really trying to punish me this time.

I groan as I roll out of bed, my shoulder aching and reminding me of the shitty game I played yesterday. This whole conflict with Jessie is fucking with my game, and I've got to get it under control right fucking now or this season's gonna be my worst one yet. It's probably my last, so I need to make it count.

I push my marriage issues to the back of my mind and get ready to hit the gym. It's an off day, but I need to at least stretch out this arm. Possibly hit the treadmill and get rid of some of the fog clouding my brain from fighting with my wife.

I find Bailey making a smoothie in the kitchen when I journey downstairs. He looks up at me and studies my face, like he's trying to read my mind or some shit.

"What, man?" I ask gruffly. I'm not in the mood to chit-chat.

"Nothing," he says, but it doesn't sound like nothing. "How was your night?" He's looking at me again. Way too intensely. He knows something.

"Shitty. You?"

"Alright. I talked to Leens..."

"You talked to your fiancée? No way," I deadpan.

He's clearly looking for information, which makes me suspect Jessie went to Leena after we talked. *Shit.* She must be more pissed than I thought if Bailey's looking at me like I'm a bomb that might explode any minute.

"She said Jessie was at open mic last night. It was a rough night..."

I blow out a big breath and give up on keeping my shit to myself. "Yeah. We had a bad phone call. Jessie's never been this pissed before. It's gonna take some big groveling to get her over this one."

Bailey stares at me again for a long moment, waiting to see if I'm going to add anything.

"Dude, spit it out," I snap finally, my nerves shot.

"Leena was under the impression you guys are separating." He winces as he dumps his smoothie into two cups.

Fuck fuck fuck. She really told the girls she was leaving?

I thought this would blow over in a few weeks. The threat to leave me was just her taking her anger out on me. Trying to punish me for going back on my promise.

"She's mad. It'll blow over in a few weeks. When the girls come for WAG Weekend, we'll get everything worked out. It'll be fine." I speak with a confidence I don't feel, but Bailey nods and gives me a wary look. He knows things have been tough and is taking mercy on me and dropping it.

"I hope so, man." He claps me on my good shoulder and hands me a cup with half of the smoothie he made as he leaves the kitchen.

"It'll be fine," I whisper again to the empty kitchen, trying to loosen the knot clenching in my gut. The one that tells me maybe it won't be fine.

Another week creeps by with no word from Jessie, and a deep sense of dread has taken up residence in my chest. My game is still shit, and now Bailey keeps shooting me sympathetic glances. We're hanging out on the couch in our living room after a brutal game, watching reruns of an old sitcom. He's got an icepack wrapped around his knee, and I've got one covering my shoulder. This is our typical routine during spring training, but the quiet between us has turned awkward instead of the companionable silence we usually have.

He clears his throat and takes a drink of his Gatorade. "So, have you heard from Jessie?"

I sigh and pinch the bridge of my nose. "No. She won't take my calls and doesn't answer texts." He hums in response, as if it were exactly the answer he expected. "Has, um, has Leena told you anything?"

He shifts uncomfortably on the couch and swallows hard. "Yeah. They... Well, they moved Jess into the apartment over the Songbird this week."

"Fucking hell," I grit out. A sharp pain radiates through my stomach. "Why would she move out when I'm not even there?"

"Something about not wanting to be in a big house full of memories and making sure she was gone by the time you got back. She, uh, didn't tell you she was moving out?"

"I haven't talked to her since... since the night she said we were over. I thought she was   extra pissed. Punishing me..."

"Is that something Jessie usually would do? Say stuff just to upset you without meaning it?"

No.

"I don't know, man. *Fuck.*" I sit and stare blankly at the TV, trying to figure out how we got to this place. "I know she was pissed. I get it. She wanted me to retire, but I didn't. But is it worth throwing away almost ten years of marriage? What the fuck was I supposed to do? The team needed me."

"Yeah, but maybe Jessie needed you, too. And you didn't exactly give her much warning."

"I know, but... goddamn it!" I drag my hands through my hair. "Breaking things off over the phone? Moving out while I'm gone? Not answering when I call and text? She's fucking with my head, man."

"She probably didn't want to drag things out."

"Are you guessing or is Leena feeding you this shit?" I snap at him. "Maybe they're   giving you fake info to fuck with my head."

Bailey straightens in his seat at my harsh tone and frowns at me. "I know you're not implying that my fiancée is lying to me. It's fucking insulting to both Leena and Jessie."

"I—"

"No. You made this mess yourself. You've been stringing Jessie along for years with this hope of life after retirement. You're the one who didn't discuss your plans with her. You're the one breaking promises. I fucking told you when you showed up, you shouldn't be here, but you only heard what you wanted to. You don't get to call my girl a liar because yours finally had enough of your shit."

Bailey storms out of the room and clomps up the stairs to his room, leaving me alone. His words echo through my mind. I drop my head into my hands and think about the way Jessie looked at me when I left.

I convinced myself she wasn't that pissed, that she'd get over it. I'm starting to think her calm defeat when I walked away was worse than her screaming at me. But on the phone, she said she loved me. If she still loves me, there still has to be hope for us, hope I can fix this.

When she's here in a couple of weeks, I'll spend the whole weekend groveling. I'll woo the shit out of her. We'll make this WAG Weekend our new start. We'll get through this and be even stronger on the other side.

From the Anniversary Journal of: Dan & Jessie Chase

Year Two

Hers:

Another crazy year down! We moved again, which was stressful but ultimately for the best! Dan was traded, so we picked up and moved to Charlotte!! The best part of this move is we now live only 15 minutes away from Marlene!

I know a lot of women have trouble with their mothers-in-law, but not me. I'm so happy to get to spend so much time with her. She's filled the void where my own mother's presence should have been. Even when we were on good terms, my mom was never this caring and invested, so it's been really wonderful growing so close to Marlene.

I was a little bummed to give up my job with Michelle in Indy, but I think I'm ready to open my own business anyway, so I guess it was good timing. Working for myself is so awesome. I've already done a wedding and a baby shower to glowing reviews. Hopefully, this will be the beginning of a bright future for JC Events! Dan mentioned again that I didn't need to work if I didn't want to, but he doesn't get it. I need something for myself outside of being a baseball wife.

The Charlotte team is so great. Dan's made some good friends on the team, and the WAGs are amazing. It's hard spending so much time apart during the season, but it's been wonderful to live in such an awesome city. The other WAGs have been helping me spread the word about my business, and we all take care of each other. I miss Annie and Leena like crazy, but it's only an eight-hour drive back to Fort Starling or a quick plane ride, so it's not too bad. We all knew we'd eventually have to go our separate ways, and our friendship is strong enough to endure long-distance.

Getting traded was a bit scary, but I'm so happy with where we landed! Our house here is gorgeous. Dan didn't want to help decorate again. I know it's not really important to him, but it would have been fun to make some decisions with him. Marlene helped a ton, but I was still bummed Dan wasn't interested.

Since he's never going to look at this journal, I think I can be honest and say it doesn't always seem like Dan's interested in what I do. I'll talk about the house, the WAG friends I've made, updates on Annie and Leena, or plans for my business. I tell him all about everything going on in my life while he's on the road, but sometimes it doesn't feel like he's actually listening. He makes noises like he is and nods, but I can tell his mind is elsewhere. He's under a lot of pressure with a new team, but it sometimes makes me kind of sad that he doesn't seem to care more about what's going on with me.

We did go on an amazing vacation to Europe this year during the off-season. Dan called it our belated honeymoon and we spent three amazing weeks seeing all of the places on my bucket list! It was such a beautiful time and I felt like we really reconnected while we were away. I've been trying to hold onto that feeling throughout the baseball season but it sure is tough! I can't wait for the offseason!

Anyway, overall, this year was fantastic. Looking forward to another awesome year with my soulmate!

XO, Jessie

His:

Chapter Five

Jessie

WHEN I WAKE TO my phone ringing, I expect it to be Dan again. Even though it's been over two weeks since we spoke, he's been calling and texting regularly. I've been ignoring them, but I don't quite have the heart to block his number yet. We'll need to have more discussions about our separation, but I'm holding off until he's home. I can't handle another phone call.

I glance at my phone and I'm surprised to find Marlene's name on the screen. I wasn't sure if I'd hear from her now that I'm leaving her son. I take a deep breath before swiping my screen to answer.

"Hey Marlene," I say, trying to keep my voice neutral.

"Hi, honey! I was wondering what weekend you're visiting Dan at spring training? I was thinking of flying out to catch one of the games, but I don't want to intrude on your weekend!"

I sit in stunned silence for a moment as I take in the fact that Dan has not told his mother we're separated. Of course, he's leaving me with the dirty work. It's very typical of Dan. He doesn't do anything he doesn't want to do.

"Oh... um... have you not talked to Dan?" I mumble into the phone.

"I talked to him a couple of weeks ago, but he was busy and rushed me off the phone before I could double-check the weekend! Why, what's up?"

I blow out a big breath as I pinch the bridge of my nose. The wine headache and roiling nausea I'm sporting from last night are making this conversation so much worse.

"Um... Dan and I are, um, separated. I... I moved out of the house."

There's a long silence on the other end of the phone. I even pull the phone away from my face to make sure the call is still connected.

"Marlene?"

"I'm here, sweetie," she says softly. "Are you okay?"

Her kind tone has me instantly in tears. "Not really," I croak out.

"I'm sure. You've been together for a long time. He knows, right?"

"Yeah. I told him a couple of weeks ago. I couldn't wait until he came back from spring training. I know it was probably selfish of me, but—"

"Jessie. You don't need to explain yourself to me." She takes a deep breath, and I can hear her exhale across the phone. "I knew when he told me he decided not to retire after all, it would cause problems. I'm so sorry it's come to this."

"Me too." I let out a shaky breath. "I want you to know... you've been the best mother-in-law I could have asked for. You've been the mother I always wanted, and I'll never forget it."

"Oh, honey. I'm not going anywhere. I don't care if you're divorcing my son, you're the daughter I always wanted, and it'll stay this way."

A sob bursts out as I start to cry in earnest. Her mention of divorce sends a sharp stab of pain through my heart. I know it's the next step, but I still haven't wrapped my head around the idea.

"I'm sorry. I'm a mess."

"Completely understandable, honey. This is not an easy thing to go through. Is there anything I can do?" I hear her sniffle. This is probably hard for her, too, and it helps me get a grip on myself.

"No. Thank you, though."

"Okay, sweetie. But I mean it. I'm not going anywhere. You call me if you need me, okay?"

"Thanks, Marlene. Love you."

"Love you too, Jess."

I'm happy Marlene doesn't seem to hate me, but everything will still be different between us. I collapse back on the bed and let the sobs take over my body again, the fatigue of the last few weeks weighing me down. Who knew leaving your husband would be so exhausting? It's like I could sleep for weeks and never feel rested.

I knew when I decided I was done giving Dan chances, it would hurt, but I underestimated just how much. My whole body aches with the pain of separating my life from his. I let myself wallow and cry until I drift back to sleep.

I collapse onto a barstool right in front of Cass and rest my head on the bar top on a random Wednesday night a week later. It's been over a month since Dan left for spring training. I haven't spoken to him for almost three weeks, although he's still been calling and texting. I can't bring myself to answer him.

I'm honestly surprised he hasn't given up. I gave Leena the go-ahead for Bailey to tell Dan I moved out. I know I'm being a coward, but I'm barely hanging on over here. It's like leaving Dan has made my whole body shut down. I'm exhausted, emotional, and nauseous all the time.

I'm sure we'll have it out when he's back, and I'll officially ask for a divorce. I have yet to actually say the word out loud. It feels so big, so final. For now, the idea makes my stomach turn. Cass looks at me sympathetically when I finally lift my head to look at her.

"You alright?" she asks kindly.

"Not really. Can I have some Sprite? My stomach is all wonky today."

She nods and moves to grab a glass, filling it with the clear bubbly pop that I'm hoping will settle my stomach. She sets the glass in front of me.

"Here you go. Have you eaten anything?"

"Not really. Everything sounds gross."

"I get it. My stomach's all fucked up right now, too." She winces as if she's in pain, resting a hand on her lower abdomen. "Fucking period. Does it need to make me fucking miserable for a solid week? You've done your job letting me know I'm not knocked up, now be on your way. Right?"

Her words are like a bucket of ice-cold water over my head as I do the math.

"Fuck," I whisper, eyes wide and staring at Cass.

"What? Whoa, Jess, you okay? Do you need a bucket or something?"

"I...I..."

"Hey, put your head between your knees. Let me get you a trash can."

I do as she says because I can't seem to catch my breath. I'm full-on panicking because I'm suddenly realizing I haven't had a period this month. I've been so stressed with everything, I didn't even think of it.

Until now.

"Jessie? Jess?"

"I think I'm gonna be sick." I heave a couple of times over the small trash can Cass handed me, but nothing comes up. My mind races as I scramble to remember when my last period was. I can hear Cass talking in a concerned voice, her phone up to her ear.

"We're gonna go to Leena's. C'mon, I'll drive you."

"What about the bar?" I murmur, letting her help me off my stool. I clutch the trashcan to my chest in case I need it.

"Alaina just got here to take over. I'm off."

I stop in my tracks. "Wait. Can you take me to my house? Tell Leena to meet us there?"

"On it." She shoots off a text message, and we both wave at Alaina as we step out into the cool March evening.

I spend the entire car ride trying to take deep breaths and keep the panic at bay. Surely my period's late because of all the stress. We'll get to my house, and I'll use the tests I stashed all those weeks ago. It's gotta just be stress, right?

Leena and Annie pop out of Annie's mermaid blue-green car as we pull up to my house. I sit and stare at the front for a few seconds before I get out and head toward them.

"Hey, babes, you okay? What's going on?" Annie asks as she wraps me in a hug.

"Cass said you were freaking out. What's wrong?" Leena adds.

I take a deep breath before answering them. "My period's late. Like, weeks late. I wasn't paying attention to it with everything going on. I have tests here. I... I don't know what I'm gonna do if—"

Leena and Annie wrap me in hugs from either side. The pressure of their arms around me helps to curb some of my panic.

"Everything is going to be okay," Annie murmurs in my ear, resting her chin on my shoulder.

"But what if—"

"It doesn't matter what the test says, you'll be okay. We've got you," Leena whispers on the other side, and I take a stuttering breath. We stand clutching each other until my breath comes a little easier, and I give them both a nod. They step back but stay close to me as we walk up the front path.

I unlock the door with shaking hands and take a deep breath to bolster myself before stepping through the doorway. I haven't been back to the house in a couple of weeks, and the air is stale. I flip on the lights as I make my way up to my bathroom to grab the bag I stashed under the sink when Dan left for spring training, thinking I'd never need it.

I look up in the mirror and see Leena and Annie standing behind me.

"You guys gonna stay in here while I pee?" I snark, trying to break some of the tension.

Leena shrugs, "We've been best friends for almost twenty years. Pretty sure we've peed in the same room before."

Annie huffs out a laugh. "Especially in college."

I roll my eyes and laugh with them; it feels good to lighten the mood a bit.

"Fine, stay if you want!" I rip open the packages and take a glance over the instructions before taking the test. "Make yourselves useful and set a timer for three minutes," I call out as I click the plastic lid back onto the plastic tube.

I set the test, the one that now feels like a ticking time bomb on the edge of the tub, and cross the bathroom to wash my hands. I study my face in the mirror as I wait for a little piece of plastic to confirm what I already know. What I knew the instant I realized my period hadn't shown up. All the signs are there; I've just been writing them off as signs of stress.

What the fuck am I gonna do?

How am I supposed to do this with a man I've just left? All along, I didn't want to do the baby thing alone while he traveled. Now I'll be doing it completely alone. The universe is not my friend. Talk about kicking a girl while she's down.

The alarm on Annie's phone jolts me out of my spiraling thoughts. I walk back to the tub and grab the test. I blow out a big breath before looking down to see the two lines clear as day.

Shit.

"Jess? What's it say?" Leena asks softly. I look up at her with tears filling my eyes.

"Positive," I croak out through the tears. "I'm having a baby. Alone."

The calm of seconds ago evaporates, and I let out a sob, which has both of them jumping up to resume their comforting positions on either side of me.

"Hey, you are not alone. We will be here with you every single step of the way," Leena declares.

"Absolutely. We have your back, Jess," Annie adds.

"Ugh, how did this even happen?" I groan with my eyes clenched.

"If you don't know how babies are made by now, you have bigger problems," Cass's snarky voice echoes from the doorway.

"Cass!" Leena scolds, eyes wide and darting back and forth between me and Cass, worried about how I'll react. But Cass's snark is exactly the dose of humor I needed to make me feel a little better about my newest life-altering crisis. I throw back my head and laugh. Annie and Leena tentatively let go of me, still worried but unable to keep from smiling at my peals of laughter, which have caused a different type of tear to roll from the corners of my eyes.

"Thanks, Cass. I thought you left, but I'm really glad you didn't." She smirks and shrugs at me. I want to hug her, but her closed off, arms crossed, body language tells me it's not a great idea. "C'mon, I'm hungry, and I just thought of something my stomach doesn't hate the idea of."

I find a box of Kraft macaroni and cheese in the pantry and get a pot of water boiling on the stove. As I'm waiting for the noodles to cook, I zone out and find myself remembering exactly how this baby situation happened.

I'm putting away laundry when Dan walks into our bedroom, already pulling off his sweaty workout clothes.

"Hey, Babe! How was your workout?" I chirp as I hang a dress in the closet. "Did Bailey take off?"

Bailey's been coming over to work out with Dan in our home gym a couple of days a week now that Dan doesn't use the Flash facilities as much. The two of them have been attached at the hip for the last few years, I don't think either of them likes to work out without the other. It'll probably be hard for them to adjust to being apart when Bailey heads out for spring training in a couple of days.

"It was fine. My shoulder's still touchy." He rolls his shoulders a bit, wincing. I'm glad he retired, with how bad his shoulder pain has gotten. The team doctor seemed to think he'd need surgery at some point, but Dan put it off, not wanting to be on the injured list during the season, but maybe now he'll get it taken care of.

His eyes catch on the pair of underwear I'm folding into my dresser, and I can see the instant he's stopped thinking about his shoulder and starts focusing on a different body part. I slow down with the next pair, making sure to hold them in the air longer.

It's funny how, after ten years of marriage, just putting away the laundry can become foreplay. I fold myself in half to open the bottom drawer of my dresser to put away a pair of jeans. Unsurprisingly, Dan moves to press himself against my ass, his large hands gripping my curvy hips. I press my hips back into him, and he lets out a low growl.

"Wanna shower with me, Jessie Baby?"

"I think I could probably be persuaded," I reply, turning in his arms and giving him a mischievous smile. "What's in it for me?"

"A couple of orgasms?"

"Hmm, add in a duet at open mic tonight and you have a deal."

"How about I just go to open mic and cheer when you sing?"

"I don't know... I really want to do a duet!"

He studies my face for a moment before countering, "Three orgasms now, loud cheering, you can get tipsy with the girls, and we'll have teenager car sex when we get home?"

"Oh, Mr. Chase. You know me so well! Deal."

He chuckles as he pulls my top up over my head. "I'd hope, after thirteen years, I'd have you figured out."

My laugh turns into a sharp inhale as he kisses a path down my neck. His hands move to unbutton the jeans I'm wearing, sliding his hand along my belly before pulling them down, taking my underwear with them. He pops open the clasp of my bra, and we let it drop to the ground between us. He ducks his head to take one of my nipples into his mouth, and I let out a soft sigh.

"Let's go, wife. In the shower, before I take you here on the floor of the closet."

"Not a bad idea, but another time when you smell better." I turn to walk away towards our bathroom, putting some extra swing into my naked hips as I go. He follows quickly and lands a playful swat on my ass.

We laugh our way into our huge tiled shower as it fills with steam from the two giant rain shower heads we had installed. Dan quickly washes the gym sweat from his body, and I make a point to stand and stare, studying his muscular body as I roam my hands over my body. Even after all these years, this man does it for me. I mean, it doesn't hurt that he's a professional athlete, and it's literally been his job to stay in shape. It's one perk of living the WAG lifestyle. Now that he's retired, I get more of the perks and less of the shitty parts, like him being gone for half of the year.

Dan blinks the water out of his face to find me staring, and his eyes spark. He stalks across the few feet of tiled floor between us and backs me against the shower wall. I hiss at the feel of the cold tile against my back. His turquoise eyes sparkle with mischief as he captures my mouth in a searing kiss.

"Starting without me, Jessie Baby?" he says as he uses one hand to pin my hands over my head against the wall.

I moan into his mouth as the fingers of his free hand find my hard nipples, alternating between them, rolling and pinching just how I like. He lowers his head to take one in his mouth and continues to knead the other breast, knowing exactly how sensitive they are.

He drops my arms to slowly lower himself to his knees in front of me, and a gasp escapes my lips as he kisses his way down my belly and across my hip bone. He finds my aching clit immediately, but doesn't give it the pressure I need right away. He dances around where I need him with his fingertips before he finally lowers his mouth to my center, causing me to cry out when he licks a path along my entrance.

"Oh God, right there!" I moan as I run my hands through his wet hair. He hitches my leg up over his shoulder and swipes his tongue across my throbbing bundle of nerves. He enters me with two of his skilled, long fingers, crooking them just right to hit the spot he knows will have me shrieking in no time.

"Fuck. Don't stop, please," I whimper before alternating between calling out for God or moaning Dan's name.

"Come for me, baby," Dan growls before latching onto my clit and giving it a hard suck.

I shatter into a million pieces, my one standing leg giving out. Dan holds me up as he lowers my leg back to the ground and kisses his way back up my body until he's standing in front of me, his rock-hard erection pressing against my stomach.

"There's one. I need to be inside you, Jessie. I'll come with you this time."

He slides me up the shower wall, and I wrap my legs around him as he enters me hard and fast. He gives me just a second to adjust to his size, but I can already feel the flutter of my inner walls telling us both my second orgasm is within reach.

A loud sizzling sound in front of me snaps me out of my memories as I realize the pot of noodles is boiling over.

"Shit!" I reach for the spoon to stir them and turn the dial down.

"You good, Jess?" Leena asks, her worried face studying me.

"Yeah. Just lost in thought," I mumble back.

"Here, why don't you sit down and let us handle the cooking for right now?" Annie says as she guides me onto one of the countertop barstools.

I blow out a big breath. My mind still circles back to that day. It's no wonder I got pregnant between the shower sex, our second round half an hour later when I tried to get dressed, and the wild quickie we had in the back of my SUV when we got home after open mic.

I press my fingers into my eyes to try to get rid of the images. I was so happy. I thought I was getting a glimpse of what our life would look like while we enjoyed his retirement and tried for a baby. How did everything go so quickly off the rails?

Leena clears her throat, and I look up at her. "Have you thought about how you're gonna tell Dan?"

I sigh. "I haven't gotten there yet. We're not even speaking right now. I haven't talked to him since I ended things a few weeks ago. I really don't want to call him now just to drop another bomb on him."

All three of them nod as they think about the situation I've found myself in.

Now it's Cass who clears her throat before asking, "Have you thought about maybe not keeping it?" She eyes me nervously, like she's afraid she's overstepped.

"It crossed my mind for a moment when I was waiting for the test," I admit in a soft voice. I give her a sad smile, and she looks less nervous. "But I've always wanted kids. It may just be a cluster of cells at the moment, but I'm already attached to the baby it'll be. I'm glad I have the right to choose, but my choice is keeping it."

"I had to ask. We'll all support you no matter what," she says in a softer voice than I've ever heard her use.

My eyes tear at such a heartfelt sentiment coming from Cass. I'm seeing why Leena has always been close with her, and now I'm hoping Cass and I can be better friends. She certainly stepped up for me tonight. I reach out and squeeze her arm.

"Thanks, Cass. I'm glad you're here."

She clears her throat again and looks uncomfortable, so I change the subject back to my crumbling marriage.

"I'll tell Dan, but I think I want to wait until he's back from training. It's only three more weeks, and it'll give me some time to wrap my head around the idea of co-parenting with him."

"So you don't think you'll get back together now?" Annie asks.

I shake my head and frown. "I don't think a baby is a good enough reason to stay in an unhappy marriage. Not when I have the means to leave. There would have to be some drastic changes on his end for me to consider trying again."

Leena nods. "Fair. I'm sure Dan will be a supportive co-parent. You guys can figure it out."

"Just... don't say anything to him next weekend. It all needs to come from me."

"Next weekend?" Leena scrunches her face. "What are you talking about?"

"Isn't WAG Weekend next weekend?"

"Jessie. There is no fucking way I'm leaving you here to go to WAG Weekend. Especially now," she says in a forceful voice.

"Leens, you don't have to do this! Bailey's gotta be dying to see you!"

"I miss Bailey with all of my heart, but I'm not leaving you while you're going through all of this. It's already done."

I burst into tears for the millionth time tonight, and they wrap me up in a group hug again. Cass even reaches out and squeezes my arm.

I have the best friends in the world. This baby and I... we're gonna be okay.

From the Anniversary Journal of: Dan & Jessie Chase

Year Three

Hers:

This has been the best year yet!! We're loving life in Charlotte, Dan's doing amazing on the team, and my business has taken off! I have so many events booked, I had to hire two other staff members to help me run them all! We're doing so, so well!

Marlene and I have gotten so close over the last year. It's been nice to have a mom here in Charlotte, especially since I still don't really talk to mine. I call my parents every so often, but the conversation is stilted and awkward. It's their own fault they're missing out on our lives here. They chose to cut me off for following my heart, and I'm not sure I'll ever forgive them. They tried to use their money to control me, and I've shown them I never needed their stupid money. The only thing I've ever wanted from them was their love and attention. I don't think I'll ever get it, and it breaks my heart.

I wish I could talk to Dan about it, but I think it would make him feel guilty that our marriage was the tipping point with them. I chose him, and he would be even harder on himself about providing if he knew what I'd given up to be with him. He's already so focused on the money side, I don't want to add any pressure. I don't care about the money. I just want to be happy with him.

In other news, my best friend here, Gwen (she's married to the Charlotte pitcher!), just had the most adorable little baby boy, and oof do I have the baby fever! He's the sweetest little thing, and I want one of my own so badly. My biological clock has officially come to life and started ticking at me loudly. But we're not quite ready for parenthood. I want to get the business a little bit more settled before we jump into adding a baby. Maybe in the next year or two, we can start discussing growing our family!

Honestly, it would be kind of hard to do it all with Dan gone so much. He already misses so much of my daily life for six months of the year, and even when he is here, it sometimes feels like he's not. He's so focused on baseball. Which is fine; it's his job, but I wish sometimes he could clock out and leave it. He brings his work home with him, even if it's just in his mind. It would be a bit crazy to add a baby to the mix!

I know tons of other WAGs are just fine doing the whole pregnancy/kid thing solo for those months, but I low-key hate the idea of him missing out on some of those earliest experiences. I love him so much, and having cute little mini-Dans running around would be incredible, but I think we'll wait a bit longer!

What a wonderful third year of marriage to the love of my life! I can't wait to see what this next year has in store!

XO, Jessie

His:

Chapter Six

Dan

"HEY, MAN, DO YOU know when the girls are getting here?" I ask as I move through the living room to grab a water out of the fridge.

Bailey looks up at me from the couch like I'm insane. "Dude. They're not coming," he snaps.

"What do you mean they're not coming? Like, WAG Weekend was canceled?" I ask, confused.

"No, most of the wives are coming, just not Leena and Jessie."

"That doesn't make any sense. Jessie's never missed a WAG Weekend." Bailey stops and stares at me for a long moment, his brow furrowed. "What?"

"Are you really this dense, or are you in some kind of denial?"

"I—"

"Your wife left you. She told you point-blank your marriage was over. She moved out of your house. Why on earth did you think she was still gonna come visit your ass here? She's not. And because your soon-to-be ex-wife is a wreck, my fiancée refuses to leave her side to visit me. You're basically fucking over everyone here." He stood up from the couch halfway through his rant and was shouting at me by the end. He's breathing hard as he stares me down with his hands planted on his hips.

"I thought this was just a big fight we were having. That she needed to cool down, and we'd go back to normal." I groan.

Bailey pinches the bridge of his nose in frustration and blows out a big breath. "Dan, I love you like a brother, so I'm gonna tell it to you straight. You need to get your head out of your ass and go home."

"I can't just leave!"

"Yeah. You can. You're not under contract. You're basically here as a favor to Coach. Plus, you've been playing like shit. If you want even the slightest chance at saving your marriage, you need to get out of here."

I swallow hard. Bailey's not kidding around. If anyone knows what Jessie is thinking, it would be Leena.

Saving my marriage. *Fuck.* I knew deep down this wasn't just another fight. I haven't talked to Jessie in weeks. She doesn't return my phone calls or texts. She said we were done and cut off all communication. I stuck my head in the sand and hoped she'd get over it.

"Shit. I gotta go. I'm gonna call Coach while I pack my shit. I don't want to burn the bridge, but you're right. I gotta go home."

Bailey huffs out a big breath and looks relieved. "Thank fuck. I was gonna kick your ass and force you onto a plane if this went on much longer." He claps me on the back and shakes his head. "When you're ready to go, I'll drive you to the airport."

"Thanks, man."

I hustle out of the room, determination filling me. I've been so stupid, waiting around here, hoping Jessie was working her way to forgiving me.

I just hope it's not too late to fix things.

Six hours later, I'm sitting in the back of a town car, riding from the Columbus airport to Fort Starling. Of course, because it's March in Ohio, I landed to find half a foot of snow on the ground and more coming down, making the hour-and-a-half drive take an extra hour. But I'm finally almost home, and my anxiety is reaching an all-time high. I tip my head back against the seat and close my eyes, replaying this crazy day.

As soon as I realized I needed to go, I called Coach and started throwing my shit into my suitcase. I blamed my shoulder and used the excuse of wanting to give it a rest and see my PT at home, but I'm pretty sure he knows something else is up because he was almost too nice about me leaving. I could practically hear the pity in his voice as he wished me luck. I want to be offended that my marriage issues have become the team gossip this season, but I'm just relieved he didn't bitch me out for bailing.

I gave Jessie another call right as I boarded my plane, but of course, she didn't answer. I considered texting her to let her know I was on my way home, but I decided against it. Maybe if she's surprised, she'll be more likely to be happy to see me. I'm not gonna give her extra time to make a list of reasons to shut me down.

The four-hour flight felt like a fucking eternity. I tried to read or play games on my phone, but mostly I stared out the window at the clouds below, thinking of Jessie.

Am I already too late?

I kept trying to call her in the weeks after that awful phone call, but I should have come home the minute she said she was done. Bailey is right, I should have immediately dropped everything to fight for her. I don't know what the fuck I was thinking letting it go on like this. These last few weeks with no word from her were torture.

I sense a change in the car's movement, and I look up in time to see a line of red taillights ahead of us. The driver tries to slow down, but I feel it the moment he loses control of the SUV. The next thing I know, we're rolling. I lose track of how many times the car flips over, flinging me around like a rag doll.

My entire world is crunching metal and shattered glass, and then, searing pain. I picture Jessie's face one more time, regretting not coming home sooner, before everything goes black.

Chapter Seven

Jessie

"YOU WANT A SPRITE? How ya feeling?"

I shoot Cass a grateful smile as I plop myself onto a barstool. I worked a ladies' luncheon at the country club today, and I'm exhausted.

"That would be great. I need the sugar to make it to bedtime."

"You're pregnant. You can go to bed whenever you want, and nobody can say a damn thing," Leena snarks at me as she comes down the bar to chat. I huff out a laugh and roll my eyes as I sip my Sprite. "How's my little niece or nephew doing?"

"Making me constantly nauseous and hate all food. I thought my stomach was all fucked up from the turmoil of leaving my husband, but nope. Just the little going-away present he left me with." Leena cringes and squeezes my hand. "My doctor said everything's looking good, and the munchkin's measuring right around eight weeks, which is what I thought based on when Dan and I were last together before he left."

My heart pinches when I think about how happy I was that day, thinking he was retired and we were ready to start building our post-base-ball life. Now I'm not speaking to him, living in a tiny apartment over a bar, and going to baby doctor visits all by myself. I shake my head to clear the depressing thoughts.

"I'm due on Halloween."

"Spooky," Cass deadpans.

Leena rolls her eyes. "Don't call my little munchkin spooky!"

"I see you're already fully embracing becoming an auntie," I smirk at Leena. For being the snarky one of our group, she's turned into quite the softie this last year.

"If I count Bailey's niece and nephew, I'm already an auntie. His brother Griffin just moved here, so you'll see them around soon!"

"Just what we need in the bar. More children."

Leena swats Cass playfully with a dish towel, and they both laugh. My phone rings, and I reach for it in my purse. My brow furrows as I read the caller ID.

"What?" Leena asks, spotting my confused look.

"It says Fort Starling General. Maybe my OB ran my blood test through the hospital?" I shrug and swipe to answer the call. "Hello?"

A professional-sounding woman responds, "Hello, is this Jessalyn Chase?"

"Yes, it is."

"I'm calling from Fort Starling General. We have you listed as the emergency contact for Daniel Chase?"

"Um, yes, he's my husband. What's going on?"

"Mr. Chase was brought into our emergency department following a car accident not long ago. We are still doing some testing, but his injuries appear to be extensive, and he will likely go into surgery soon. It would be best if you made your way into the hospital."

My mind feels like it's exploding, and my pulse is racing, but I stammer out, "Oh my God. Okay... I'm on my way. I'll be there as soon as I can."

The kind-sounding nurse signs off after giving me instructions for where to go when I get to the hospital. I'm left staring at the phone in my hand, not quite believing what she told me. The questions fly through my brain as I try to process the information. Dan's here in Fort Starling? Why isn't he still in Arizona? And more importantly, how badly is he hurt?

I look up to see Cass and Leena's worried faces. I'm getting tired of them looking at me with those expressions. Leena comes around the bar and grips my arm.

"Jess. What's going on?"

"Dan's here, and he's been in an accident. I have to get to the hospital." I stand and grab my purse. I dig for my car keys, but Leena grabs my hand.

"Let's go. I'll drive."

We hurry out to Leena's car, and she quickly gets us on the road.

"I didn't know Dan had left Arizona. I'm gonna call Bailey."

I nod, and she clicks Bailey's contact. Her phone rings through the speakers of the car before the call connects.

"Shit, sunshine, I'm sorry! I was gonna give you a heads up, Dan was on his way to win Jessie back, but I—"

"Hey, Bail, there's been an accident. Dan is in the hospital here in Fort Starling. Jessie's here with me on speaker. We're on our way to General now."

The line is silent for a long moment. "Fuck. Is he... Do you..."

"We don't know how bad it is yet," I murmur. A lump keeps my voice trapped in my throat. I attempt to clear it. "The nurse on the phone just said his injuries are extensive and he'd probably need surgery."

"Shit."

We're all silent for a minute, processing the little information we have.

"I'll call you back when we find out more, Bailey."

"Okay, sunshine. Thanks. Let me know if there's anything I can do from here... or if I need to come home. I'll get on a plane today if I need to."

I zone out as they say their goodbyes, wondering if I've said my last goodbye to Dan. We may not be speaking right now, and I may have decided to leave our marriage, but the idea of him not being in this world fills me with icy dread. Especially now that there's a baby in the mix.

Fuck. The baby. What if I never get to tell him?

"Dan doesn't even know about the baby," I choke out before a sob bursts from my chest. Losing all sense of the tense calm I had before, I let the tears flow.

Leena grips the steering wheel as she maneuvers us through the snow that's still falling. "You'll tell him. He's going to be okay, and you'll tell him about the baby."

"You don't know that. What if he—" I mumble through my tears.

"Hey, until we have information, we're going to stay positive. We're not gonna do the 'what if' thing. He's going to pull through and get to meet his little baby."

I nod and grip the handle of the door so hard my knuckles turn as white as the snow flying past the car window. I don't voice them, but my mind is still swirling with all the possibilities that could await us at the hospital. This was not what I was expecting for the next time I saw Dan.

I was dreading our next conversation, but now I'm just praying we get to have one.

Five long hours later, I'm camped out in an uncomfortable chair next to the hospital bed of my unconscious, but still alive, estranged husband. He looks somehow smaller in it, with tubes sticking out everywhere, covered in bandages and bruises. He looks terrible, and I almost lost what was left in my stomach when I first caught sight of him. The doctors are expecting Dan to make a full recovery, but he's got a long road ahead of him. I can't help thinking it could have been so much worse.

In addition to a surgery to remove his ruptured spleen and make sure there was no other internal bleeding, he'll be having another surgery on his arm in the next few days. His right arm is broken in several places and was dislocated. The doctors said his arm was trapped in the mangled car door in the accident and had to be cut free from the car.

Right now, he's sedated to let his body rest and heal. Leena and Annie are camped out in the ICU waiting room. The girls aren't allowed back here since they're not family, so they've settled in down the hall with Eric, Annie's boyfriend. Leena said Bailey let the team know about the accident and is on his way from Arizona. The girls refused to leave the hospital since I refused to leave Dan's side. Separated or not, I'm not leaving him right now.

A sharp gasp from the doorway catches my attention, and I look up to see Marlene hovering just inside. Instantly, the tears start back up at the sight of the woman who's been more of a mother to me than my own. I stand as she moves toward the bed.

"He's gonna be okay," I croak out. She lets out a tight sob and comes over to squeeze his hand. "They just have him sedated to help him rest and heal." I told her as much when I talked to her on the phone a few hours ago, but I think we both need to hear it again. Especially with how rough he looks.

She turns her attention to me and walks around the hospital bed to pull me into her arms. I break down into sobs at her comforting touch.

"Oh, sweetie. It's gonna be okay. I've got you."

Her tenderness overwhelms me. She knows I left Dan, but she's still here comforting me while her son lies unconscious in a hospital bed. The thought turns my stomach, and the stress of the night hits me all over again.

"I'm gonna be sick," I murmur as I run for the tiny bathroom attached to Dan's room.

Marlene follows me in, holding my hair and rubbing my back as I lose the little bit of food I've eaten in the last twelve hours. When my stomach is empty, I wash my hands and splash some water on my face. I rinse my mouth out and pop a piece of peppermint gum to settle my stomach before dropping back into my chair next to Dan's bedside.

"Sorry," I mumble, catching Marlene's eye.

"Honey, don't be sorry. I'm sure this has been stressful. I'm glad you were here for him."

"Of course." I blow out a big breath. "Dan and I may not be in a great place right now, but I couldn't leave him here alone. Especially not with…"

I pause, not sure if this is the best place for Marlene to find out she's going to be a grandma.

"Not with what, dear?" She pulls a second chair around to sit next to me and reaches out to hold my hand.

"Not with the big secret I haven't told Dan yet. Well, it's technically a little secret right now, but it's getting bigger every day." I place my hand over my still-flat tummy and give her a shrug, and she immediately understands what I'm saying.

"Oh, my God. This is the best news I think I've ever heard." She pulls me into her arms. When she pulls back, she studies my face, tears spilling from her eyes. "You're gonna make me a grandma?"

I nod through my own tears, touched by her joyful reaction. Let's hope Dan's as happy about this recent development as his mom is.

"I wanted to wait to tell him until he was back from training. It was bad enough that our last conversation was me ending our marriage. I couldn't drop another bomb on him over the phone."

"Understandable. So how far along are you? When are you due?"

"Just about eight weeks. I'm due on Halloween."

"Easy to remember! Oh, I'm so happy. I know this is complicated for you guys, but a grandbaby is a dream come true." I smile at Marlene. She's gonna be the best grandma in the world. Her smile falters a bit. "Is there a chance you and Dan can work things out?"

"I don't know." If she asked me yesterday, I would have said no, but now? I'm not so sure. After everything I felt when I thought Dan could be gone, my thoughts are muddled.

She hums in response. "You have to do what's best for you and the baby."

I nod and give her a sad smile. We sit holding hands as we watch Dan sleep, listening to the beeps and hums of the hospital.

Could I give Dan another chance? Give us a chance to be a happy family? Bailey said he was here to win me back, but what does that even mean?

All I know is I'm here with him now, and I'm not leaving again until he is back on his feet. I'll help him while his body heals and then decide if we can heal what's broken between us.

From the Anniversary Journal of: Dan & Jessie Chase

Year Four

Hers:

It was a rough one this year. Dan got traded again at the end of last season, moving us from Charlotte to California. Not gonna lie, I was devastated. Everything was in Charlotte. His mom, my business, our friends. It was still a manageable drive or a quick flight to Fort Starling and in the same time zone as Leena and Annie. Now we're clear across the country from everyone.

I moved JC Events here, but since so much of wedding and event planning is word of mouth, it's been pretty slow-going to get clients booked. It feels like I had to start over from scratch. It's the same business, but other than some great reviews from clients across the country, I had to start from square one. Luckily, my staff could finish out my Charlotte events with me only flying back a few times, but of course, now they both had to find new jobs. I miss them. I miss everyone.

Leena got engaged this year. I met him when we were home for my birthday and the holidays, but I guess I haven't gotten to know Adam very well because we did not click. I think he's kind of an asshole, but Leena seems happy. Gram hinted she's not Adam's biggest fan, and Annie hates him. I wish I were there to help Leena plan or figure out what's going on with this guy.

It's been six months here, and it's awful. The WAGs here are different. They're snobby and bitchy. They look at me like I shouldn't be there, even though I am just as much a baseball wife as they are. I bet if I told them I come from money, they'd stop turning their noses up at me, but I don't even want to use my parents' money in that way. I don't need their reputation any more than I need the stupid trust fund.

Luckily, Dan's doing great with the new team. His stats have been fantastic. His transition has been a lot easier than mine, that's for sure. He knows I've struggled, and I can tell he feels guilty, but not guilty enough to spend any extra time at home with me or helping me decorate.

We went on an amazing Caribbean cruise just after New Year's. I wish it could be the off-season all the time. He's so attentive when his mind isn't on baseball. We have so much fun together, but I feel like I have to stock up on attention during those few months off to get me through the season.

He mentioned retiring the other day, and I was surprised. We've never discussed the end of baseball before. He pointed out he's getting older (crazy how being almost 30 is old in baseball years), and he probably won't be playing too much longer. He promised that when he retires, we'll be able to spend way more time together. We can live wherever we want. I'm not sure he realizes that if he were more present the whole year, it wouldn't matter where we live or if he retires. I just want him to be here when he's here.

He brought up the possibility of having a baby soon. He said having a baby to focus on might help here, but I don't want to do all the pregnancy and baby stuff alone. I have no support here. Maybe when he retires would be a better plan. I'm only twenty-five, we have plenty of time!

Long entry this year... hopefully next year has a happier report!

XO, Jessie

His:

Chapter Eight
Dan

I CAN HEAR JESSIE's voice. She doesn't sound pissed off at me, so this must be a dream. There's an annoying beeping sound keeping me from hearing what Jessie's saying. Fuck, my head hurts. My whole body hurts. Maybe this isn't a dream. My bad shoulder is on fire, the ache radiating from a bone-deep level and shooting pain all the way to my fingertips. My chest and side ache, too. What the fuck is happening?

It's my mom's voice that finally snaps me out of the fog and gets me to open my eyes. My head is pounding. Swiveling to look around the small hospital room makes my vision start to spin.

"He's awake," my mom says quietly. "Dan, honey, try not to move."

She leans into my vision, tears shining in her eyes. I clear my throat, another thing to add to the list of things that hurt.

"Jessie?" I croak out.

"I'm here, Dan." She comes along my mom's side, and they switch places. Jessie grabs my hand. "Your mom's gonna get the nurses and get you some water. They had to intubate you when you first got here, and for surgery, so your throat might hurt."

I give her the tiniest nod I can, trying to keep from making the pounding in my head any worse. I clear my throat a few more times, cringing at the sandpaper feel. Jessie moves a lock of hair out of my forehead and gives me a sad smile.

"You're here," I say in a raspy, weak voice.

"Of course, I'm here. We're still married, Dan. Even with…everything, I wouldn't have left you here alone." She squeezes my hand.

"Can we… I came home to—"

"We can talk about all of that when you're feeling better." She gives me another sad smile as she pats my hand. I want to say more. I want to beg for forgiveness, tell her how much I love her, but my head is swimming and words won't come out of my aching throat.

"Mr. Chase, it's good to see you awake." A kind-looking doctor says as he enters the room wearing dark blue scrubs and a white coat. He's tall, probably around six feet, with greying dark brown hair. I'd put him in his fifties. "My name is Dr. Vincent. Do you know who you are, where you are?"

"Hospital?" I rasp out.

"Good, any idea what city?"

"Fort Starling?"

"Very good." I keep answering his questions about the month and the president, and he nods along. "You have a minor concussion in addition to your other injuries. Common in collisions like yours. You may have a headache for a few days, possibly sensitivities to light and sound. It should all clear up on its own."

I give him another small nod. My head already feels better than it did when I first woke up, but that may have to do with a nurse pushing some meds into my IV on my left arm.

"Onto your more extensive injuries, your spleen ruptured in the collision, so we had to remove it and clean your abdominal cavity. We did not find evidence of other internal injuries. Your right arm is fractured in three separate locations, and your shoulder was severely dislocated. We were informed by first responders that it was pinned in the wreckage."

"Fuck," I murmur.

Dr. Vincent gives me an encouraging smile. "I know it's a lot to take in. We're going to give your body a few days to rest and heal. We'd like to see some of the swelling go down and give your system a break from being sedated. After that, they'll operate on your arm again. We'll clear some scar tissue in your shoulder and set all fractures. You'll likely be here with us for the next couple of weeks so that we can monitor all of your injuries."

"Will he get his full range of motion back?" Jessie asks quietly.

"That'll be something to discuss with the orthopedic specialist. I'm giving you the rundown of everything the departments put together, but I'm a general surgeon and I wouldn't want to make promises ortho can't keep."

He answers a few more questions, but I'm struggling to keep my eyes open. Whatever the nurse gave me must be the good stuff because before I know it, I'm drifting off. The last thing I see is Jessie standing next to my bed, holding my hand.

A few days later, I wake from a nap to Jessie's voice. My head is clearer now, so I'm able to make out the words, even though she's sitting in a chair farther away from the bed.

"Thanks for covering for me, Charlie. The seating chart is in the Anderson Wedding cloud file," Jessie says into her phone. Her hands are clicking away at her laptop. "No, just make sure that the mom and aunt are at separate tables so they don't have drama…"

The room goes quiet as Jessie listens to Charlie. "Leah, the bride, said the shower will be a good test run for the actual wedding since the space is smaller. She may un-invite the aunt if they can't handle their shit."

Whoa. The wedding they're working on sounds like it could be a shitshow. Is it always like that?

"Perfect, thank you so much. We'll be here for at least another week, and then I think he'll need some help once we get him home."

My ears perk up even more now that they're talking about me. I shouldn't eavesdrop, but I'm desperate to know where Jessie's head's at.

"I don't know, Char. We haven't talked about it yet."

I strain to hear anything from the other side of the phone, but the only thing I can hear are the sounds of hospital machines.

"Yeah. I'm here until he's back on his feet, and then I don't know. Everything's kind of up in the air. It's so fucking complicated now."

Shit. That does not sound good for me. I was hoping the fact that she was here by my side meant she was gonna give me another chance, but it sounds like she's just here out of some marital obligation, and that stings. But on the other hand, she's here. She's clearly missing work to be with me, just like she has over and over throughout the years. Fuck, have I ever thanked her for it?

When I hear her say her goodbyes and disconnect the call, I clear my throat and use the remote by the bed to move to a more upright position. Jessie closes her computer and comes to sit in the chair closest to me.

"Do you need anything? Let me grab your water."

"Thanks, baby," I say after a long gulp of water. She tenses at the endearment but nods. "Do you need to be at work?"

"It's fine. Charlie and Sam are covering my events until you're back on your feet. I can make sure all of the behind-the-scenes stuff is done from here. Besides, we have your next surgery tomorrow, so I should be here for that."

"I'm glad you're here. Can we... can we talk about us?" I ask quietly.

Jessie blows out a big breath, and her gaze shoots to the floor. Not great signs for me. "Dan, let's not do this here. You should be focusing on getting better. We can talk about us when you're healed up."

I want to argue with her. I want to push her to talk now, but I'm afraid that if I push her too hard, she'll bolt. She clearly doesn't want to have this conversation. I have to follow her lead since I'm already on the brink of losing her.

"Okay, Jess. We can wait." She nods her head and sits back in her chair. "You know I love you, right?"

She looks up and meets my eyes. "I know, Dan. I love you too."

I'm relieved to hear her say the words, but I see the pain and torment that cross her eyes. She still loves me, but she's not sure she wants to. The thought knocks the wind out of me, and I'm thrilled to see my mom walk in moments later, breaking the awkward silence between us.

Jessie takes my mom's arrival as a reason to make her escape. She says she's off to shower and grab some non-hospital food, but I can see that she's trying to get some space from me. My eyes follow her and linger on the doorway where she just vanished.

"How ya doing, honey?" my mom asks as she takes the chair close to me.

"My whole body still hurts, I'm freaked about this surgery, and I'm not sure if my wife is still leaving me," I grumble.

"Well, that about sums it up."

"Has Jessie said anything to you about what she's thinking?" I ask, my tone pleading.

"Oh, sweetie, even if she had, I wouldn't betray that confidence. This is something you're going to have to work out between the two of you. I know she's feeling conflicted. The very fact that she dropped everything to be by your side says she still has some feelings for you, but I know she was serious about you separating before the accident. Which I am not happy about hearing from her instead of you, by the way."

I groan. "I know, Mom. I was in denial. I thought I'd be able to work things out and I wouldn't have to tell you anything was ever wrong."

"Not taking her seriously was your first mistake. Probably one you made long before she decided to leave you." Mom raises her eyebrows and gives me a pointed look.

"What do you mean?" I ask, pinching the bridge of my nose. My head is hurting more the longer we talk about all of this.

"It seems to me you've never taken what Jessie really wants seriously. You tend to do whatever you want, hoping she'll go along with it. It worked for a while, but I do believe she's done with that."

I nod and lean my head back against the pillows. Mom pats my hand and sits back in her chair, focusing on the color-by-number game she likes to play on her phone. I pretend to sleep, but my mind is whirling with everything my mom pointed out.

On some level, I can see that she's right. I've prioritized my baseball career over everything else, but it was for a good reason. I want to provide Jessie with the best life possible. Doesn't that count for anything?

I get that she wanted me to be done with baseball. She wanted me to pay more attention to the things she's into. But is all that really enough to give up on the years we've spent together? Enough to give up on the vows we made to each other?

I'm not so sure. Maybe she's right to push the conversation until I'm feeling better. Because when the time comes, I'm gonna fight for her to give us another chance.

Chapter Nine

Jessie

"JESSIE! YOU'RE HERE!" LEENA calls out from the end of the bar as I enter the Songbird from the apartment. The room is nearly empty since we're in the late afternoon lull between the morning coffee crowd and the evening drinkers. I smile at my friend as she wraps her arms around me. "How you holding up, babes?"

"I'm okay, hanging in there. I came by to grab some fresh clothes and real food. Snuck in a nap, too. Spending every waking hour at a hospital is exhausting."

"I bet, well, come sit for a bit." She ushers me over to a barstool, and Cass pours me a Sprite that I take with a grateful smile. "How's Dan? When's his next surgery?"

"Tomorrow morning. I'm gonna head back there for a few hours tonight before visiting hours are done."

"Have you guys discussed things yet?"

"No, he's tried to bring it up a couple of times, but I'd rather not get into it until he's back on his feet. I haven't dropped the bomb about the baby yet. I want him to focus on getting better."

"Makes sense, but it's gotta be hard on you, keeping everything in." Leena's eyes are full of concern. I give her a sad smile.

"Marlene knows everything. Having her here has been amazing. I don't know what I'll do when she has to go back to Charlotte."

"You'll let us help," she says sternly. "We're here for you, Jess. Seriously, anything you need."

"Thanks, Leens. Now, how have things been around here?"

"Pretty quiet, especially with baseball season kicking off. Bailey's been stressed trying to focus on pitching while being worried about Dan."

"Bailey's such a green flag," I say with a grin. "Good thing I set you up with him, hmm?"

Leena rolls her eyes like she does every time I brag about my excellent set up skills. "Yeah, yeah, we're eternally grateful."

I laugh and turn to look at Cass. "You wanna be my next matchmaking project, Cass?"

"Not a fucking chance," she deadpans with a glare. "I don't do relationships."

Leena and I both chuckle. "Fine! Whatever you say," I say with fake sincerity.

She rolls her eyes and disappears into the back. Leena's eyes are still trained on my face.

"You're gonna try to set her up, aren't you?"

I shrug. "If I find the right person for her. I can't think of anyone off the top of my head that could go toe to toe with Cass."

Leena huffs out a laugh. "You're right. It would take a special person for that."

"I'm sure he's out there. Anyway, I should get back to the hospital."

"Okay, babes. Take care of yourself and let me know if you guys need anything."

I assure Leena that I will and get another big hug before heading back to the tension of sitting at the bedside of a man I'm not sure I still want to be married to. I know Dan wants answers. He wants to know where my head's at, but I'm still so unsure.

In the moments when I didn't know how badly he was hurt, I was terrified that he wouldn't make it. I couldn't take the thought of a world without Dan in it. I wanted more time with him. I wasn't ready to say goodbye.

But I'm not sure those feelings justify putting aside everything about our marriage that led to me leaving. Those problems aren't gone just because he's injured and helpless. Between the baby and Dan's recovery, I might be willing to give him another chance, but he's the one who has to make changes.

I can't survive on empty promises anymore.

After a second surgery on his arm and two full weeks in the hospital, Dan was finally released to go home. He hasn't brought up our separation since before his second surgery, but I can sense him watching me every so often. He looks like he's afraid I'm going to disappear at any moment.

Marlene insisted on getting the house ready for Dan to come home, so she's already there while we're getting discharged. Bailey drives up to the exit to help Dan into the car while I gather up the bags we've collected.

I only left a handful of times to pack some things and check in with my employees; otherwise, I've been by Dan's side. We may not have spoken about our separation, but I can still feel the distance of it between us.

The house smells somehow both amazing and nauseating as we step through the door. Bailey escorts Dan up to our room so he can lie down. The trip from the hospital was enough to wipe him out. I stop in the kitchen to say hi to Marlene and put off being in our bedroom with Dan. It's like returning to the place where we fell apart, and I'm not ready.

"Hi honey, the lasagna just finished, and the garlic bread will be done in a few minutes. Any of that sound good to you?"

"I'll have some of the bread; I'm not sure I can stomach the lasagna," I say, my nose crinkling at the sight and smell of the bubbling dish.

"First trimester's a bitch, huh?"

I glance at the doorway of the kitchen guiltily. I still haven't told Dan about the baby. It just seemed wrong to pile on when he was in so much pain. I'd like him to have a clearer mind when I drop such big news on him. Now that we're home, it's probably time.

"I'll take it up to him when it's ready." I point to the tray Marlene's been putting together for Dan. She nods at me, smiling.

"I've loaded up your freezer with meals for the next couple of weeks, and I did a load of grocery shopping, so the fridge is full too. I'm going to stay through this weekend, then I've got to get back to Charlotte."

I sigh. "I really appreciate all of your help. We're going to miss you."

"Don't you worry, I'll be back." She studies my face for a moment before adding tentatively, "I'm actually thinking about moving up here."

"But you love Charlotte!" I exclaim, stunned. "Why would you move?"

"I do love my city, but I'm gonna love being a grandma even more. I don't want to miss it."

I burst into tears. Fucking pregnancy hormones. "That would be amazing. We would love to have you here."

She wraps me in a hug, only letting me go when the timer for the oven goes off. She finishes loading up Dan's tray and puts a small plate of garlic bread on it for me. She mentions needing to take a shower and vanishes to the suite we built at the back of our house for her when she visits. Maybe she could live there full-time. It would be so helpful to have her here when the baby comes, and I never did like the idea of her living alone.

I shake my head, waving the thoughts away. It's a discussion for later. I don't even know if I'll be living in this house when the baby comes. Everything is so up in the air at this point. I grab the tray and head upstairs, knowing that when I get there, it's time to have a conversation with Dan.

Chapter Ten

Dan

EVERYTHING FUCKING HURTS, BUT I'm glad to be home in my own bed. Now, if only I could get my wife to talk to me. She said we would discuss things when I was better, but it's driving me crazy having her near but still so far away. I can sense her holding back. It's like she's gone while she's still right in front of me. The only thing worse would be her actually being gone, so I've kept my mouth shut.

Bailey helped me get situated while Jess went to talk to my mom. He's been shooting me sympathetic looks since the accident, but I'm not sure if they're for my injuries or whatever he knows about what Jessie's thinking. I'm sure Leena gave him the inside scoop, but I don't want to put him in the middle more than he already has been.

Once he takes off, I try to nap, but I can't stop my thoughts from spiraling back to the last conversation Jessie and I had in this room. The last place I saw her before everything fell apart. It's like a fucking crime scene.

I hear steps outside the door and find Jessie with a large tray carrying the scent of my mom's lasagna into the room. I sit up, propped up by the headboard and pillows, so she can set the tray across my lap. Jessie situates herself next to me on her side of the bed. I'm glad to see she plans to stay, but I frown down at the tray as I notice there's only one plate of lasagna.

"Are you not gonna eat?" I ask her. My concern about the weight she's lost in the last few weeks returns full force. I noticed it right away at the hospital, and she picked at any food she had while we were there. "You've barely eaten anything since I've been back."

She offers me a fake smile and grabs the tiny plate of extra garlic bread off the tray.

"This is mine. I'm not feeling lasagna."

"Jessie, that's not enough. Seriously, here, have some of my lasagna." I try to push the lasagna towards her, and her face goes pale.

"Shit," she mumbles as she throws a hand over her mouth. She's up and running toward the bathroom before I can even put my plate back down. I can hear her throwing up, but I'm slow getting up from the bed. I curse my injured body. I finally make it to the bathroom door, as she's flushing the toilet and standing up.

"Do you need anything? Are you okay?"

She shakes her head as she's washing her hands and rinsing out her mouth at the sink. "I'm fine, Dan. You shouldn't be up." She ushers me back to the bed, but I'm still concerned. She settles back on the bed and picks at the piece of garlic bread like nothing happened.

"Jessie Baby. What's going on? Are you sick? Did you pick up a bug at the hospital?"

She scoffs and takes another bite of bread. "It's not a bug." She blows out a big breath and looks me in the eye with a serious expression. "I'm pregnant."

"You're... holy shit. But we... Are you sure?" I stammer out.

Pregnant. I did not see that one coming.

"I'm sure," she says with a laugh. "I hit ten weeks yesterday."

"So, it's..."

"Dan Chase, I swear to God if you ask me if this baby is yours, I will murder you in your sleep."

I huff out a laugh, glad some of my Jessie's sass is returning. She's been too polite to me these last couple of weeks.

"I was gonna ask when it's due. I'd never accuse you of cheating."

She gives me a sharp nod. "We may not have been together this last month and a half, but we are still technically married. I wouldn't do that."

Her words leave a painful mark on my heart. While I was living in denial over our last conversation, she was sure we were over.

"Are we still not together?" I swallow hard. "I came back early from training to fix things between us. Am I... Is it... Is it too late?"

She sighs, and my stomach clenches at the frown on her face. "I don't know."

"Even with the baby coming?"

"A baby isn't a good reason to stay in an unhappy marriage."

Ouch. Her words sting in ways I never would have expected. Obviously, we have big enough problems that she wanted to leave me, but to have her call our marriage "unhappy" cuts deep.

"Jessie, please. Can we..."

"Dan, let's focus on getting you well. I'm not going anywhere while you're recovering, and we can just... figure out where we're going from there."

I don't love her answer, but beggars can't be choosers, so I nod. "Okay, but let me say this. I love you. I will love you forever, and I can't wait to meet our baby."

She sniffs and gives me a teary smile while pulling her phone out of her pocket.

"Here, I have something to show you."

She pulls up a video on her phone and turns the sound all the way up. The picture shows a screen with a black background with a white, blurry, bean-looking thing in the middle. A fast whomping sound comes out of the phone as the video starts over again. The bean squirms on the screen, and all the breath leaves my body.

"Is it—?"

"Yep, it's the munchkin's heartbeat."

"Oh, my God." My eyes fill with tears as we sit and watch the video play over and over again. I sniffle and wipe my eyes. "Fuck. This is amazing."

Jessie lifts her teary gaze at me and gives me the first actual smile I've seen on her face since I've been back. I hate the unsteady ground we seem to be standing on, but fuck am I proud of what we've created, even if it doesn't look like much yet.

"I'm sorry I wasn't here to go with you," I say, but I can instantly feel that it was the wrong thing to say. She stiffens and pulls away from me a bit.

"Sure," she says with a nod. There's no hostility in her voice, but I get the feeling that she doesn't believe that I'm sorry I missed the first appointment.

"Seriously, Jessie. I wish I had been there." I'm a little surprised to find that I really mean it. I wish I had been there. "You were right all along that I wouldn't want to miss these appointments."

Her eyebrows shoot up, and she studies my face as if she's trying to decide whether or not to believe me. Finally, she clears her throat and nods. "I'm due on Halloween," she murmurs, putting her phone down.

"So we've got plenty of time." I study her again with new eyes, seeing the weight loss and the exhaustion lining her eyes in a different light. "I'm guessing you haven't been feeling great?"

"No. I'm nauseous all the time, and most foods make me sick just thinking of them. I haven't thrown up much, but I always feel gross and exhausted. I've lost some weight instead of gaining it. My doctor says it's normal and gave me some ideas of things I could try. With your accident, I haven't had a chance."

"We'll stop at the store after my PT appointment tomorrow, or we can just order it and have it delivered. We'll make sure you have what you need to feel better."

She nods and leans back into the pillows. She's looking at the TV playing sports highlights, but her eyes look far away, like she's lost in her thoughts.

I'm ecstatic about the baby news, but it's making me nervous; she's still so unsure of where we stand. What would even happen if she decides to leave again? I don't think Jess would ever keep my child from me, but she's clearly the one who knows what she's doing with a baby.

What if I'm shit at the whole dad thing? What if Jessie decides she can find a better partner out there, and I become the part-time dad while someone else lives with them full-time? If I can't fix things, there's a chance I might end up watching my kid's life from the visitor's dugout, and fuck if it doesn't scare the shit out of me.

"Give me five more of those, then you can be done," Eric says while watching the range of motion in my bad shoulder. It was already fucked up before the accident, and now it hurts like a bitch. The doctors said they think I'll get my full range of motion back, but I'm pretty sure baseball is done for me. They haven't given me an answer, but it doesn't look good, and it's making me a surly asshole to think of it.

"Fuck, Doc. You're a sadist, and you know it."

Eric chuckles and smiles at me. He's been my friend since college and my PT for the last several years, so he's not fazed by my bitching. He shakes his head at me and makes a note on his iPad. "Just doing my job, dude."

I grunt out a response as I finish the reps he asked for. He hands me a bottle of water and places an ice pack on my shoulder.

"How's everything? Incisions all healing up?"

"Yeah. I'm still pretty sore, but everything's healing." It's been a rough week since I got home from the hospital, and I know I've been a grumpy bastard. I can hear myself being a dick to Jessie, but I can't seem to stop it.

"How's Jessie doing with everything?" His blue eyes are calculating as he studies me, telling me right away he knows about the baby but isn't sure if I know. Another thing to add to the list of things pissing me off about our whole situation. He probably found out about the baby before I did. *Fuck*. I bet Bailey knew before I even left Arizona.

"She's okay, I guess," I say, deciding not to engage with him on baby talk. He stares for another minute before he gives up. Once again, I know I'm being an asshole and can't bring myself to quit. "I'll see you later, man."

He nods at me and pats me on my good shoulder. Eric and I have been friends for thirteen years, so he's not gonna let my shitty attitude faze him now.

I stomp myself out to the car, where Jessie is waiting for me. She said she had work to do during my appointment, but I'm guessing she wanted a break from me. She closes her laptop as I slump into my seat and buckle the belt.

"How'd it go?" she asks once I'm settled.

"Fine."

I can see her staring at me out of the corner of my eye, waiting for more information. When I don't say anything more, she shakes her head and puts the car in gear. I can see her jaw clench as she bites back whatever she wants to say.

I wish she'd just say it already. I'm itching for a fight, and I can feel it coming. This battle's been coming since she bailed on our marriage. If we weren't headed straight to the orthopedic specialist for a follow-up right now, I'd lean into it, but I have a suspicion this fight will take more time than the ten-minute drive will allow.

We park at the doctor's office and get out of the car in the same icy silence we've been driving in. I walk ahead and leave Jessie to follow behind.

We don't talk for the whole fifteen minutes we sit in the waiting room, and we don't talk while we're sitting in the exam room.

Dr. Gupta finally breaks the silence when he knocks and enters the room. He's a middle-aged Indian man who speaks with a crisp British accent even though he's lived in the States for thirty-plus years. He comes in smiling and shakes my hand and Jessie's hand before plopping down on his rolling stool.

"Hello, Dan, Jessie, how are we today?" he asks in a chipper tone, which only serves to annoy me. I know he's going to give me bad news, so I wish he'd knock off the friendly catch-up tone.

"Doing alright," I grit out.

He nods seriously, sensing my tone. He does a quick exam of my shoulder, testing my range of motion and inspecting the cast covering my lower arm. He pulls up the results of the MRI I had a couple of days ago. Finally, the doctor clears his throat and sits back a bit on his stool to meet my eye. I know what he's going to say before it ever comes out of his mouth.

"It looks like your shoulder and the fractures in your arm are healing well, Dan. You should regain the full range of motion and use of your arm." He pauses, like he's hoping I won't ask my next question.

"And baseball?"

I see Jessie flinch out of the corner of my eye, but I don't dare focus on her. I don't want to see how happy she'll be that I have to retire now.

Dr. Gupta gives me a sympathetic look as he shakes his head. "Dan, I'm sorry, but considering your injuries and your age, I wouldn't recommend you return to playing professionally. The likelihood of your being able to perform at the level needed is slim to none. I'm sorry."

Fuck, that hurts.

I knew when I woke up in a hospital bed, my baseball days were over, but hearing it confirmed still breaks my heart. Baseball has been my life for over thirty years, and now I'm just supposed to be done?

I see Jessie wipe a tear from under her eye. What the fuck is that about? Why is she crying like she didn't want my baseball career to end? Is this some sort of joke?

I nod my head at the doctor as he gives me info about taking care of my arm and follow-up protocols, but my mind is already racing to get out of here. He shakes my hand and pats Jessie on the shoulder before leaving us in tense silence. I get up and walk away again, leaving Jessie to follow.

She stops at the window to schedule my next follow-up, but I don't even stop. I head straight to the parking lot, the crisp April air helping to cool my head a bit. We drive home in more tense silence. I make it two steps into the house before I can't hold back any longer.

"What was with you in there?"

"What do you mean?" Jessie asks, looking confused and startled by my harsh tone.

"What was with the fucking tears, Jess? I'd think you'd be thrilled my baseball days are over."

I see the moment she decides she's not putting up with my shit. The time has come; this fight has been brewing for weeks. Now it's here, and I'm not sure I'm ready for what it will bring.

From the Anniversary Journal of: Dan & Jessie Chase

Year Five

Hers:

Five whole years. Half a decade married to my favorite person! This year was better than last year. I still hate California, but at least I feel a little more settled. Luckily, business has picked up, and I'm busy enough to even hire an assistant, Carley! She's awesome, and it's been so nice to have a friend here. Not nearly as close as I was to Gwen in Charlotte, or Leena and Annie at home, but at least I'm not alone all the time now.

The other WAGs are still mostly bitchy; a few of them will at least make polite chit-chat at games, but I don't really fit in with their group. Most of them don't work outside of being baseball wives. They've made being a WAG their entire job, their entire personality, and it's fine for them, but I like having something for myself outside of Dan's job. I think it's because Los Angeles is such a different type of city from Charlotte.

Dan hurt his shoulder early this season, so he's been in PT a lot in the last few months. It's been nice having him home more often, even though I hate it when he's in pain. He's pretty much made recovery a full-time job, so he's still out at PT and workouts pretty often, even if he's not traveling with the team.

I tried to bring up the idea of him making more of an effort to be present during the season, and he said he'd try. I wish I could say there was much of a difference, but it lasted maybe a couple of weeks. It's something I've been thinking about for a while now, and finally got up the nerve to say something, but it didn't do any good. Apparently, he can only put in the effort during the off-season. It's like I have a loving husband half of the year, and a friends-with-benefits roommate the other half. LOL

Sometimes I think he says things just to get me to leave him alone, not because he really means them. A head pat to keep me quiet and happy. Like the whole retirement thing. With his shoulder injury, he said he's not likely to play much longer, but the team doctor says he'll be able to rehab it fully, so I'm not holding my breath about him retiring. He doesn't really want to; he just thinks it's what I want.

He brought up having a baby again, but I would really rather wait until he's retired. Even though things are better here now, I still don't have enough support to add a baby. I don't want to do everything completely by myself. Even when he's here, his mind is somewhere else. Why would I want to add being pregnant to our current dynamic?

I don't need him to rush retiring just for us to have babies. I'd hate for him to leave baseball before he's ready, and I can wait. They can come along later when things are a little more stable between us. When he has time to spend with us year-round. We have time!

Can't wait to see where the rest of this decade leads us!

XO, Jessie

His:

Chapter Eleven

Jessie

THE WEEK SINCE DAN was discharged from the hospital has been the longest of my life. The first few days were fine. Dan was in pain but still relatively happy to be back home with me. Then something shifted. His mood has been dark. He snaps at me more often than anything else, and I'm just about at the end of my patience.

I'm nauseous, exhausted, and emotionally overwhelmed by being here with him. So if he wants to fight. I'm ready. I have years' worth of grievances I was too sad to voice before. I was ready to let them go and walk away, but now he's coming at me with a growly voice and a sneer on his face, so I guess we're doing this. I mentally crack my knuckles and steel myself for the fight of my life.

"Are you implying that I'm happy you were hurt?" I ask in a low voice.

"I'm not implying it. I'm saying it straight out. You're happy I can't play ball anymore. You're thrilled I'll be trapped here in this house with you and our kid and not playing the game I've loved my whole life."

My head snaps back as if he'd slapped me, and pain clenches my heart. Trapped with me and our kid? Is this really what he thinks his life will be like now that he's retired?

"Well, that explains a lot. I understand now why you couldn't stand to retire. I didn't realize spending time with your family, a family you wanted and pushed for by the way, would be such torture," I say, my voice full of pent-up rage. We're about two seconds away from letting it all out.

"You know what I fucking meant. You wanted me to retire, and now here it is. It's like you manifested it or some shit."

Yep, there it is.

"Yeah, Dan, I manifested this fucking situation. Unplanned baby with the husband I was planning on leaving. Check! Major car accident, so husband can't play ball and needs to be nursed back to health. Check! Asshole husband treating me like garbage. Fucking check! Manifestation success!" I'm practically screaming at him by the time I get to the end of the list. I'm not putting up with his shit anymore.

"Just admit you still have one foot out the door. I begged you to give me another chance, but you're still ready to leave me."

"A lot of good you're doing with the extra chance, Dan. You've been treating me like shit for days now. Barking at me when you need something. Never saying thank you. Never giving a fuck about how I'm doing," I snap at him, bracing my hands on the edge of the kitchen island.

"I'm dealing with a lot right now, Jessie. My career is over, just like you wanted."

"And I'm not dealing with a lot? When was the last time you asked me how I feel? When was the last time you asked about my work? When was the last time you considered not only am I here, taking care of you, despite things being in an awkward place with us, but I'm also running my own business and growing a human? When was the last time you thought of anybody but yourself?"

A guilty expression crosses his face just before it's replaced by anger again. "You're one to talk! You were the one who was pushing me to give up my career so you could have your version of a perfect little life. You're the one who selfishly wanted to force me to give up my dreams."

"Oh, I'm the selfish one? You're right, Dan. How selfish of me to follow you and your career through multiple moves. So selfish of me to pick up and start my entire business over from scratch each time your precious dream forced us to move. You're the one who made promise after promise, never keeping a single one."

"Speaking of broken promises, how about for better or worse, huh? You seem to have no problem breaking that one, Jessie," he yells.

"You're right. I broke a vow. Once I realized you only cared about yourself and I couldn't trust you to keep your word, I decided maybe it wasn't worth being miserable until death does us part," I scream back at him, tears pouring down my cheeks as his face contorts in anger.

"Miserable? Are you fucking kidding me? Look around this house. Look at all the things baseball has provided for you. You want to tell me you're miserable?"

"With a husband who doesn't see me and definitely doesn't care about me? Yeah, I'm fucking miserable. I never cared about the money. If I had, I wouldn't have married you. I would have moved home like my parents wanted me to and had access to my trust fund."

Dan is struck silent, and I realize my mistake. I never told Dan about my trust fund or the fact that my parents changed the terms of it when I went against their wishes to marry him. My stomach drops. This isn't gonna be pretty.

"What trust fund?" he says, eerily calm.

"My grandparents set it up when I was born. I was supposed to be able to access my trust fund when I graduated from college, but my parents threatened to change the terms if I went through with the wedding. I was hell-bent on marrying you, so my parents followed through on their threat." I shrug, trying to make it sound like it wasn't a big deal. Like it wasn't a relationship-ending blow-up with my parents, and the reason we barely speak to each other now.

"When?" he asks in a low, dangerous voice.

"When what?"

"When do you get access?"

"When I turned thirty, it was turned over to me. I haven't touched it."

The contrast between the silent room and the screaming fight we were having moments ago is deafening. I never meant for him to find out about the trust this way. I never meant for him to find out about it at all. I half forgot it myself since I have no intention of ever using it.

"Why did you keep it from me?" Dan finally grits out.

"Because it didn't matter. Their money would never be what I based my decisions on. I didn't want to put pressure on you when we were just starting out. You've always been so focused on living up to my parents' money."

I blow out a big breath, all the fight leaving my body. I'm tired of this back and forth. None of this fighting is worth it. It's just making everything hurt more. It was part of why I left in the first place, and this fight tonight proves nothing is going to change. He doesn't see me. He doesn't understand what I need. I'm done.

"I don't want to fight anymore," I say in a low, sad voice.

He nods and pinches the bridge of his nose. "Me neither. Let's order some dinner, and then we can watch a movie or something. We can pick up talking about all this tomorrow."

He still doesn't get it. He looks confused when I shake my head. "No. I mean, I'm done fighting, for good. I can't do it, Dan. You never seem to hear my side, and you'd rather say what you think I want to hear than actually fix anything. This isn't the example I want to set for my child." I swallow hard and force myself to look into his eyes. I can see them fill with panic. "I want a divorce."

The word rings out in the silence between us, and he lets out a noise like I've landed a punch. It's the first time I've said the "D" word out loud since this all started.

"Jessie. Please," he croaks out. His eyes are shining with unshed tears, but I can't let it stop me.

"I'm gonna head back to the Songbird. I'll keep you updated on the baby stuff, and we'll figure out how we're going to tackle co-parenting. We've got some time to work things out before the baby's here."

He follows me as I move upstairs to throw the few things I brought over back into my suitcase. I never bothered moving all of my stuff back from the apartment. Deep down, I think I knew I would be back living there once Dan recovered.

"I thought you were going to give us another chance," he snaps at me as I'm throwing toiletries into my bag.

"Yeah, how well do you think it's going? I've been giving us chances for years. I kept hanging on, hoping this was the year we'd get back on track. I'm finally seeing now it's never going to happen."

"So you're giving up?"

"You can call it what you want. I'm choosing myself for once, after years of putting you first. I'm going to finally make myself a priority. Myself and this baby. It's clear now you were never going to."

I march out of the bedroom door and straight down the stairs. I don't stop to look around. I already said my drawn-out, painful goodbye to my dream house. I get in my car and back out of the driveway. I take one last glance and see Dan standing in the bedroom window, watching me drive away.

It's been a week since I heard from Dan. I've called his mom a couple of times to make sure she's been able to check in on him, and I know from Leena that Bailey's been over there, but there's been no direct communication. I wouldn't text him now, but I promised to update him on baby shit, and I do what I say I'm going to, unlike someone I know.

Me:

> Hey, I'm not sure if you wanted to go, but I have a baby doctor appointment tomorrow at 10 am.

Dan:

> Do you want me to go?

Me:

It's up to you. I'm good either way.

God, it sounds fake even in a text. I'm not good either way. I'm bad either way. I'm shattered all over again. Any semblance of moving on I did in the weeks after ending our marriage the first time has disappeared, and I'm right back at the start.

I was stupid and got my hopes up that after a near-death accident, Dan would be able to see my side of things. He'd realize our relationship had been one-sided, and he'd be willing to at least try to make me a priority in his life. What's the whole saying about insanity and doing the same thing but expecting different results? Yep, it's me. Full on crazy.

Dan:

I'll be there.

Well, thank heaven for small miracles. Maybe he'll be able to make the baby a priority even if he didn't give a shit about me. I won't be holding my breath. I respond with the office's address and leave it there.

"I'm guessing from the frown on your face you're texting Dan?" Leena asks from behind the bar. She makes her way around to sit next to me as Cass pops out from the back with a tray of clean glasses.

I blow out a breath and slump in my seat. Annie breezes through the doorway and sits on the stool on my other side.

"Yep. Just giving him the details for my OB appointment tomorrow. I'm not looking forward to dealing with him on top of still feeling like warmed-up garbage."

"Gross," Cass deadpans at me.

"Exactly. Being pregnant is fucking awful. I'm exhausted, still nauseous despite taking meds for it, and most foods sound disgusting and make me sick. I'm surviving on Easy Mac and pizza Lunchables over here. And to top it all off, I feel like a massive bitch for complaining about it all."

"What, why?" Leena asks, her forehead wrinkling in confusion.

"How many women out there would kill to be in my position? There are so many couples out there trying for a baby. Happy couples with healthy marriages have to dump thousands of dollars into fertility treatments, and here I am complaining about my oopsie baby. I wasn't even trying to get pregnant! We weren't preventing it, but we weren't really trying. I thought for sure it would take longer than two months off the pill. Like, why me and not them? It's fucking unfair."

"It is. But the universe being unfair doesn't mean you have to love every moment of this experience. Your feelings are valid," Annie intones seriously. I raise my eyes at her words of wisdom, and she shrugs. "What? I have a good therapist; sue me."

I let out a deep sigh. "I should probably go back to mine. I was seeing her pretty consistently for a while, but I stopped when the season ended, and I thought Dan was actually going to retire. Like it was going to fix everything."

"Yeah, you may have been a bit delusional. Even if he had retired, it probably wouldn't have fixed everything in your relationship," Leena says with raised eyebrows.

I rest my head on my crossed arms as I groan, "Ugh, you're right. I'll call and see if I can get back on her schedule."

"You know, it probably wouldn't hurt for you and Dan to do some counseling together."

My head snaps up and my nose scrunches. "Why would we do that? We're getting divorced. It's too late for couples' therapy."

"True, but you guys will be connected for the rest of your lives through the baby." She points out with a wave towards my still mostly flat stomach. "You're gonna need to learn how to communicate better if you're going to co-parent."

I cross my arms over my chest at her suggestion, but deep down I know she's right. Co-parenting will already be hard enough. I wave my hand and put my head back down on the bar.

"I can't think about this right now. I'm too tired."

"It's okay. You have time," Annie says as she pats my back comfortingly. "Now, should we chat about updates for Leena's wedding?"

"Ooh, yes!" I pop back up to sitting again, always ready to discuss wedding planning. Leena and Bailey have the date set for a cozy mid-November wedding. I gasp as a thought occurs to me. "Shit, Leena! I just realized I'll be like two weeks postpartum for your wedding!"

Leena shrugs. "It's okay, babes. It works out since you're my Matron of Honor and Annie's my Maid of Honor. Plus, Cass agreed to be a bridesmaid too. We'll have things covered if you need to dip out at any point."

I scrunch my nose at the title. "I thought we agreed to call us co-maids of honor? Matron makes me sound like an old lady."

Annie snickers into her glass. "I mean, you are the oldest!"

"By three months, you skank."

Leena and Annie both laugh, and Cass shakes her head at our antics. It's a relief to laugh with my friends after the last few weeks of drama.

"Whatever your titles are, at least we now have a built-in flower girl or ring bearer."

My eyes widen as I'm hit with the fact that I will have an actual baby at Leena's wedding. I will be someone's mother. What a mind-fuck.

"You good, Jess?" Leena asks, picking up on my mood shift.

"Yeah, just weird to think of. My due date seems so far away, but it's really not."

"I can't wait!" Leena singsongs in a way so far from her usual snarky self that we all turn to look at her. "What? I'm gonna be a badass auntie! I'm finally gonna get some practice in with Bailey's niece and nephew in a few weeks."

I huff a laugh and shake my head as I think about how much things have changed in the last year. Leena was in a dark place for so long, I was afraid she'd never come out. I'm so thrilled she's doing better and found her happy ending, all thanks to me and my matchmaking skills, I might add. But I can't help feeling sorry for myself and the way my happy ending has disintegrated.

I never planned to do this baby thing by myself. The whole point of waiting until Dan retired was so I wouldn't be doing everything alone. It all feels like such a waste. I spent ten years waiting to live the life I wanted, and now I have to start over. Any future I imagined is now completely transformed. With one act of putting myself first, I've irrevocably changed everything.

I hope it was worth it.

From the Anniversary Journal of: Dan & Jessie Chase

Year Six

Hers:

Just as I got comfortable in California, Dan got traded again. All the progress I made in the last two years, gone just like that. Moving my business yet again is devastating. It's like I'm starting all over again. Back to square one, no clients, no employees. I get it; this is part of the baseball life I signed up for when I married Dan. I knew it could come with moves like this, but I definitely didn't realize just how hard it would be.

It's not all bad because we were traded to Fort Starling, and I was really thrilled to come home. It was also good timing, since we lost Leena's Gram this winter. I'm so thankful I could be here for her, especially with Annie living in Chicago now. Leens dumped the asshole, so she's also coping with a breakup and is kind of a mess.

Dan had the Flash write into his contract that he can't be traded again, so we're home for good. I had thought we'd be in California until he retired. Dan kept saying it was our last move until he was done. This time, he showed me the actual contract. It's for two more years, so his vague promises of retiring "soon" seem less reliable.

I think he's just telling me what he thinks I want to hear. We've had a couple of fights about his making decisions without me, keeping me in the dark. We had another bad one about him being more present when he's home. I don't think he makes me feel invisible on purpose, but it's low-key killing me to feel like he doesn't care if I'm here. It's like I could leave and he wouldn't even notice.

He started asking about starting a family again now that we're back home, but I'm not ready. I want him around for all the parts that go into having a baby. The doctor appointments, the deco-rating, the excitement of it all. I want him to be present enough when it's just us before we take the jump into parenthood.

I knew his schedule would be hard when we got married, but I don't think I realized just how all-consuming baseball would be. Everything else in our lives has to be built around his schedule. His dreams. Sometimes it doesn't feel like there is room for any of my interests. I haven't said any of this part to Dan. It feels selfish, and I don't want to make him feel bad over things he can't really change. I don't want him to retire before he's ready. I just want him to care about our life outside of baseball the way he used to.

Hopefully, things will get better now that we have a permanent home to build. Even if he has no interest in helping me with any of the details.

XO, Jessie

His:

Chapter Twelve
Dan

I HEAR THE FRONT door opening, and I sit up straight in the bed I've barely left since Jessie walked out. I've been going to my PT and doctor appointments, usually taking the car service since I still can't drive. Bailey came over to check in a few days ago, but otherwise, I haven't felt the need to get out of bed.

Baseball's done.

Jessie's gone.

No one is here to care if I'm eating all my meals in bed and haven't opened the blackout curtains in days. I'm sure at some point I'll stop moping and figure out what I'm supposed to do with my life, but for now I'm wallowing.

The sound of someone moving around the house sends a jolt of hope through my body. It's gotta be Jessie. Maybe she's ready to work on things if she's here to pick me up for the baby appointment in an hour.

I hop out of bed and run into the bathroom to at least brush my teeth before she sees me. As I'm walking out of the bedroom, a voice calls from the bottom of the stairs.

"Dan? You up there?"

"Mom?" I yell back, confused and disappointed. It's not Jessie. At the bottom of the stairs, I find my mother waiting for me, a large suitcase sitting next to her. "What are you doing here?"

"Surprise! I thought you could use some help until you get back on your feet."

"You can just take time off like this?" She's always been insistent on keeping her job even though I've begged her to let me take care of things. It's infuriating. What's the point of making millions if you can't spend some on the woman who raised you? Apparently, *no one* needed me to make all this money.

She waves me off. "Don't you worry about it."

"How'd you know I'd be here alone?"

She shoots me a look that says she thinks I'm an idiot, but she loves me anyway. "Jessie called me."

"So you know she left me," I say in a petulant tone.

She nods with a wince. She's always loved Jessie so much, the daughter she never had. I'm sure she's not loving this development in my marriage.

"I was hoping y'all would work things out since she was here for you after the accident and with the baby coming..." Her voice trails off, thankfully not pointing out how I had a second chance to win Jessie back, and I blew it. "Anyway, shouldn't you get changed? We need to leave for the baby appointment in half an hour."

I shouldn't be surprised my mom and Jessie are still connected enough for my mom to know the appointment schedule. Jessie's divorcing me, not my mom, but I thought she'd be more sympathetic. I should probably think about what it means that my own mother isn't on my side in all this.

I grunt out a response and head back up the stairs to get ready for the appointment. It's such a confusing combination of emotions. I'm excited to find out more about the baby and hear a heartbeat in person. But I'm dreading facing my pissed-off wife. Ex-wife, I guess I should get used to saying.

Fuck, no.

I'm not calling her my ex-wife until the signatures are dry on the divorce papers. Until then, I still have a chance to fix all this. To figure out a way to win her back.

Until it's legal, there's hope, even if it's only a tiny speck.

When we get to the doctor's office, Jessie is sitting in the waiting area, looking down at her phone. On our way over to her, I glance around the large open waiting room and find several other women, reading magazines or on their phones.

My eyes focus on a couple across the room from where Jessie's sitting. The woman's belly is large and rounded. Her partner has his hand on the bump, and they're smiling as they talk softly. My stomach clenches as I realize again what I've lost. Will Jessie and I get to do any of the expecting couple things? I regret all over again the way I pushed her to do this all alone for so many years. What the fuck was I thinking?

Jessie's eyes pop up from her phone screen as we get closer to her, and she shoots me a sad smile before turning her actual smile on for my mom. Mom plops into the chair next to Jessie and pulls her into a hug while I stand awkwardly in front of them. Mom nods to a chair across from them, and I follow her lead, collapsing into the seat with my eyes on Jessie as she sits back in her chair and puts her phone in her bag.

It's only been about a week since I saw Jessie, but I study her, looking for changes, afraid I'm gonna find out how much happier she looks without me. But she looks kind of rough. I mean, Jessie's always beautiful, but she looks too thin and has dark circles under her eyes. I thought it would make me feel better, but I'm wracked with guilt and worry to see she's been struggling.

"How you feeling, sweetie?" Mom asks Jessie softly, and I lean forward, eager to hear the answer I should already know.

"I still feel like shit," Jessie huffs out. "I'm not as nauseous as I was since I'm taking the B6 and Unisom every night, but I still can't stand to eat most things, and I'm so exhausted. I can barely make it past dinnertime before I'm ready to pass out."

"It'll get better." My mom squeezes her hand, giving her a sympathetic smile.

"I'm ready for the second trimester, for sure."

"Just a couple more weeks!"

I'm realizing how much I don't know about this pregnancy shit. Jessie told me this was her twelve-week appointment, but I don't know what it really means. When does the trimester switch? *Shit.* I'm dropping the ball on the one good thing I have left in my life. I'm such a dick, I'm seeing why Jessie wants to drop me. I'm deadweight over here, with nothing to contribute.

A nurse in light pink scrubs pops out of the door at the far end of the waiting room and calls Jessie's name. She stands up from her chair and starts to walk before pausing and looking at me.

"You coming?" she asks in a tight voice.

"Oh, yeah!" I move quickly to follow her. "Mom?"

"I'll wait right here." My mom sits back in her chair and starts playing her game her phone. Jessie and I both stare at her for a beat, like we wish she'd come back with us so we'd have a buffer. The nurse sends me to the exam room while they weigh Jessie and have her pee in a cup in the bathroom down the hall.

When she joins me in the room, the nurse takes her blood pressure and asks her a bunch of questions, tells her to strip from the waist down, and leaves a little paper blanket on the exam table. When Jessie stands up and pops the button on her jeans, I stand up awkwardly.

"Do you want me to leave?"

Jessie rolls her eyes. "Dan, you've seen me without pants about a million times."

"I know. Things are just different now," I say cautiously, sitting back in my chair. I keep my gaze trained on the floor, but I can still see Jessie out of the corner of my eye.

Jessie slips her underwear down her legs. She folds the jeans she was wearing and tucks the underwear inside, and places them on an extra chair before sitting on the exam table and draping the paper blanket over her legs. Once she settles, she looks down at me.

"Do you want to be in the room when I have the baby?" she asks softly.

"Of course, Jessie. I want to be there for everything."

"Okay, then. Seeing me pantsless in an exam room is nothing compared to the horror show you'll see in a few months. It's not a big deal." She shrugs and looks down into her lap, fidgeting with the paper blanket.

I huff a nervous laugh, and we fall back into tense silence. A few minutes later, a soft rap on the door signals the doctor, a tiny blonde woman wearing slacks and a purple sweater under her white coat. She's younger than I expected, probably only a few years older than me. She greets Jessie with a warm smile, then looks my way. She reaches out to shake my hand.

"Hi there, I'm Dr. Sharon," she says as I shake her hand, and she looks at Jessie. "Is this Dad?"

"Yes, this is my husband, Dan." My heart lifts in my chest as she introduces me as her husband. Not her ex-husband. Not her estranged husband. I'm sure she didn't mean anything by it, not wanting to explain our situation to this doctor, but I can't help the small flash of hope that ignites at the title.

Dr. Sharon perches on a stool as she asks Jessie a bunch of questions about how she's doing. The doctor assures her everything sounds normal and, hopefully, some symptoms will ease up as she gets into the second trimester, which apparently starts at fourteen weeks.

"Alrighty, let's check the heartbeat on this little one." She brings over a small device with a speaker and a tiny digital screen. The machine is connected to a wand like you see on TV, and she rolls it around in some goop she squeezed onto Jessie's still-flat stomach. The speaker makes a whooshing sound when she moves it around, but we still don't hear a heartbeat sound. The doctor keeps moving it around, and I see Jessie's eyes tighten with concern.

The doctor turns the machine off. "Baby's feeling stubborn today, we're gonna switch to ultrasound." She's still smiling and calm, but I can see a flicker of panic in Jessie's gaze. I move over to her side and grab her hand as the doctor pops into the hallway, asking someone to bring over the portable ultrasound machine. Jessie squeezes my hand, giving away just how scared she is in this moment.

Dr. Sharon gets the machine going quickly, and the screen comes to life with a little white figure that kind of looks like a little alien with a big head and tiny arms and legs. There's a quick flutter in the middle of the alien creature, and almost as soon as I think it, Dr. Sharon clicks a button, and the same galloping sound I heard on Jessie's phone a few weeks ago fills the room.

My heart clenches with relief at the sound, as the breath I definitely realized I was holding escapes. This little squirmy being is my kid. In seven-ish months, I'll be holding this little person in my arms. *Fuck*. Jessie was right about me needing to be here for every moment of this pregnancy. I never should have fought her. I could have missed all of this if she'd given in to my pushing.

"There it is. Your little one is hanging out towards the back of your uterus, so it was hard to find them with the Doppler. As they grow, we'll be able to find the heartbeat more easily without the ultrasound." She assures us everything looks good and the baby is growing at the right pace.

Jessie blows out a big breath in relief but keeps her grip on my hand. She looks up at me with glossy eyes and a beautiful smile on her face. I lean down and kiss her chastely. Separation be damned. I quickly take a video on my phone of the amazing sound. I'll be replaying it for months as we wait to meet our baby, or at least until we get to see them in another scan.

The doctor prints out a few photos of the ultrasound for us and leaves the room for Jessie to get dressed. The silence between us returns, but it isn't quite as tense as it was before.

Jessie makes the next appointment for four weeks from now, and we exit into the waiting area. My mom stands up from her chair as she sees us approaching. I pull my phone out so I can show her the video.

"How'd it go?" she asks with a bright smile.

"Gave us a little scare when the doctor couldn't find the heartbeat at first, but we got to see the munchkin with an ultrasound instead, so I'm not complaining," Jessie explains with a beaming smile.

I hand the video over to my mom.

"Oh my goodness, look how much they've grown in just a few weeks. They're like a little person now." She smiles up at me with tears in her eyes. She's gonna be a fucking awesome grandma. We head out to the cars, and just before Jessie walks away, Mom looks up and asks, "Should we grab some lunch? Jess?"

"Oh, uh..." Jessie steps back a bit like she's gonna run away, but my mom's pleading eyes make her give in. "I guess it would be fine. You guys pick where, though. This baby hates most food right now, so I'm not sure how much I'll even be able to eat."

"What about the Golden Corral? It's still there, right? You can pick and choose what sounds good to you."

Jessie looks up at me, startled. Is she surprised I want to take care of her? Or is she surprised I remember us going there all the time when we were still dating? Some of our best memories were of us stuffing our faces at the buffet.

I used to come visit her here in Fort Starling during her school breaks and when I could get away. Since I was a poor minor league player, we'd eat a full day's worth of food to get our money's worth. Have I really been that much of a jackass that she thinks I wouldn't eat at the Golden Corral with her?

"Yeah, sounds good. I'll meet you guys over there." She quickly walks toward her car. My mom and I both watch her climb into her SUV and start the engine before we both duck into Mom's small car.

"How'd it go between you guys?" Mom asks as we drive.

"It was awkward at first. Tense. Better once we saw the baby. She introduced me to the doctor as her husband. I don't know if it means anything, though. She may have just not wanted to explain."

Mom hums, a calculating expression on her face. We drive in comfortable silence for a while before she speaks up again.

"Do you want to work things out with Jessie?"

"Of course. I just... I don't know how to fix things. I know I've made mistakes, but she's kept secrets too, and honestly, I'm pretty pissed she's so willing to give up on us. It's all so fucked up."

"Would you be willing to do couples' counseling?"

I let out an enormous sigh. I see the benefit of therapy, but I've never done it myself. At this point, it couldn't hurt, though. "Yeah. If Jessie's willing to try it, I'd be willing."

"Alright, good to know. Maybe if I suggest it, Jessie would consider it. I'll feel her out at lunch."

Her eyebrows are raised in question as she parks in front of the restaurant.

"Okay, Mom," I agree, because I think Jessie is way less likely to blow off a suggestion from Mom than from me. "Let's go."

I blow out a big breath and offer a prayer to whoever might be listening that this might be the first step to fixing things with Jessie. I'm not ready to give up hope yet.

"Oh my God, I'm so full," I grumble, tempted to pop open the button on my jeans. "I can't remember the last time I ate so much."

Jessie huffs out a laugh. "Same."

I shoot her a mock disapproving look, and she rewards me with an actual laugh. "Baby, you barely ate anything."

She sucks in a quick inhale at my endearment, but shakes it off quickly with a nervous laugh. "This is still the most I've eaten in a while. This baby hates almost anything I try to eat. And when something does sound good, it's usually in the middle of the night and impossible to get."

"I was that way when I was pregnant with Dan," my mom says.

"Did it get better?" Jessie asks, desperation in her voice.

"I don't think you want to know the answer." Mom shoots Jessie a sympathetic glance, and Jessie groans.

"Ugh, no! I'm counting on it getting better in a few weeks."

"I'm sure it will, dear; every pregnancy is different." Mom pats Jessie's hand as she glances at me, and I know she's about to bring up our discussion from the car. I grip my water glass and brace myself. "Jess, there's actually something I wanted to discuss with both of you."

Jessie is instantly on guard, and I avoid looking her in the eyes. "Okay..." she replies tentatively, giving Mom a nod to continue.

"I talked to Dan about this on the way over here, and I was wondering if you would consider going to counseling. Together, I mean. Even if it doesn't lead to a reconciliation, I think it would be a good idea for you both to be on the same page. Parenting is hard enough; co-parenting after a divorce will be even more intense. It may be a good idea to work on your communication now instead of waiting until you're in the trenches of diapers and midnight feedings."

The mention of divorce takes the wind out of me. Mom is right, but I hate the way she's framing it as something to make separating easier, rather than a way to stay together.

Jessie lets out a big breath. "I think you're right, Marlene. I actually just set up an appointment to go back to my former therapist. I'll ask her for a recommendation for someone who works with couples." She looks up at me with a furrowed brow. "If it works for you?"

I clear my throat and nod. "I think it's a good idea," I say softly.

Jessie's eyebrows wing up, as if she expected me to push back. She can be surprised all she wants, but I'll do whatever I need to do to prove I'm willing to fight for us. She may be ready to give up, but I'm not.

Not even close.

From the Anniversary Journal of: Dan & Jessie Chase

Year Seven

Hers:

This year was kind of a slog. I'm so happy we moved home to Fort Starling, but man, has it been hard rebuilding my business. The whole first year home was rough. I'm just now starting to gain some traction, getting more events on the books. I may even need to hire a new assistant soon, and this time I'll hopefully get to keep them without the threat of a new trade.

Dan's still playing strong, despite his shoulder bothering him more often than not. His contract is done at the end of this year, and while he hasn't outright said he's retiring, he's hinted at it. I'm trying not to put pressure on him to retire if he doesn't want to, but I'm ready. I'm ready to have him home all year round. He's so much more focused on us during the off-season. I'm ready for it to always be the off-season. Ready for us to really start building our life here.

Maybe when he's free from the pressure of maintaining his stats or rehabbing his shoulder, he'll be a little more invested in rebuilding some of the closeness we've lost over the last few years. Lord knows he can't seem to be present at home with things as they are now. Maybe when the pressure's off, he'll remember I'm here.

It's been amazing getting to see him live out his dreams, but he doesn't really seem interested in my business or in doing any of the fun things I want to do when he has downtime during the season. He's always promised that when baseball is over, it'll be our time. For us to become the family we've always wanted.

He's been pushing harder for us to just go ahead and get pregnant, but I reminded him that kids are off the table until he's retired. Plus, I want to feel as closely bonded as we used to be, before we add being parents to the mix. I want us back before we change into new versions of ourselves. We can wait a little longer.

The house we bought here is stunning. I've had a wonderful time designing all the decor to be the perfect family home for when the time comes. I keep hoping he'll show some interest in our home.

I've saved some projects so we can do them together. He keeps telling me just to hire someone, but I don't know. I just want him to show an ounce of initiative in building our future.

Looking forward to the new adventures this next year will bring!

XO, Jessie

His:

Chapter Thirteen

Jessie

It took a couple of weeks to get into a couples counselor, but here we are at Theresa's office, ready to get started with whatever this will be. I still can't quite get a read on Dan. I was surprised when he agreed so easily to do counseling. The weeks since our OB checkup have been tense and awkward between us.

We haven't seen each other much, but he's been texting to ask how I'm doing. I can't seem to figure out whether he's trying to check on me or if he's just asking because of the baby. I don't know whether I want him to fight for us or let it go. Letting it go would be easier for my energy levels, but much harder for my heart. Despite all the disappointment and anger, I still love him, and it's fucking with my head. I'm sure the pregnancy hormones are not helping.

Theresa greets us and shakes both of our hands as we enter her office. On one side of the room, she has a large desk with a computer monitor sitting in the middle. A tall bookshelf lines the wall behind the desk. An enormous window looks out onto a forested area, giving her office a cozy, secluded vibe. There's a large sofa along the opposite wall from her desk with an armchair facing it. On the coffee table sits a box of tissues, which I'm sure I'll be needing in my current emotional state.

Dan and I settle on opposite sides of the couch, leaving a cushion of space between us. Theresa joins us, sitting in the armchair, holding a notepad and pen. She's an older Hispanic woman, maybe in her late fifties or early sixties. Her hair is a mix of black and gray curls and she has kind brown eyes behind a pair of wire framed glasses. She smiles at us as she clicks her pen open.

"So, what brings you here today?"

Dan and I share a nervous look before I clear my throat.

"Um, well... we're currently separated. I've asked for a divorce, but we're also expecting. I didn't know I was pregnant when I ended things."

"The first time," Dan interjects.

"What do you mean?" Theresa asks calmly, looking back and forth between us.

"This is the second time she's left. We got back together briefly, and she left again."

"Tell me more about how the timeline went."

I blow out a breath and explain quickly about Dan's retirement promise, his sudden departure for spring training, my decision to leave while he was gone, discovering I was pregnant, his accident, our brief reunion, and my reasons for leaving again.

"Anything to add, Dan?"

"About sums it up," he grumbles with a clenched jaw. He got more and more tense as I went through everything. He looks pissed. What does he have to be pissed about?

"It sounds like you've both been through a lot of upheaval in the last few months." She offers us a consoling smile before she continues. "I'd like to know what your goals are for these sessions. What are you hoping to get out of counseling? Dan, let's start with you."

"I don't want a divorce. I want to stay together. I'm hoping we can fix things and be a family."

I'm a little taken aback. He sounds so sure he wants to fix things, but I highly doubt he's willing to make any actual changes. I force myself to hold back an eye roll as Theresa turns her attention to me.

"Jessie, how about you?" She smiles at me encouragingly.

"I don't know. Part of me would like to work things out, if only for the baby, but another part feels like it's too late and we should just call time of death. My biggest priority is making sure our kid has the healthiest childhood possible, even if it means we're co-parenting."

Theresa nods. "A wonderful goal to have. I would encourage you to keep an open mind as we go. There's no need to make any decisions right now." I nod back at her. She's right. We have some time, and it can't hurt to explore all our options for moving forward.

"So, we've heard a bit about Jessie's reasoning for the separation. Dan, how do you feel about the separation?"

He huffs out an angry breath. "Upset. Pissed off. Confused."

"Good start. Identifying what you're feeling is important. Tell us more about how it felt to have Jessie want to end things. What went through your mind after the phone conversation while you were in Arizona?"

"I didn't believe her. I thought it was a terrible fight and she'd come around."

Makes sense considering he kept trying to call and text me during those couple of weeks. He thought if he could get me to talk, I'd forgive him and let it all go. Just like every other time he let me down, he thought he could sweet-talk me into forgiving him.

Of course, he didn't realize every time he did it, every time I let it happen, it was like sweeping broken glass under a rug. You couldn't see the problem anymore, but it didn't mean it was gone. Eventually, when you break too many glasses, you run out of space under the rug and have nowhere to hide the broken pieces.

"Had you fought like this before? Had she mentioned ending your marriage in the past?" Theresa probes with a serious look on her face.

"No," he grits out through clenched teeth. "But I didn't want to see it. It took our friend Bailey being brutally honest for me to wrap my head around the fact that she meant it when she said she was done. That's when I got on a plane to come home. I wasn't gonna let her go without a fight, but then the accident happened, and she was there. I thought she was giving us a second chance, but she left again."

I scoff. "It wasn't a second chance! It was more like a tenth chance. I've been giving us chances for years."

"But I didn't know. You never told me you were unhappy."

Theresa turns her gaze to me. "Would you say this is true, Jessie? Did you tell Dan you were unhappy with your marriage?"

I think for a beat before responding. "I guess not in those exact words, but we've been fighting over when he'd retire and when we'd have kids for years. I've been begging him to be more present and pay more attention for so long. Doesn't it seem telling that he didn't even know I was unhappy?"

"Okay. We'll get to hashing out everything, but let's table the past for a few minutes and do an exercise. I'm going to give you each a piece of paper and about ten minutes to make a list of the things you need from each other in your marriage. This could be anything from financial stability to weekly date nights. Whatever you need to feel loved and valued by the other person. Write them down and then we'll discuss."

She gives us paper and sets a timer. I go about carefully making my list. What would make me feel loved and valued? Do I even know anymore?

When the timer goes off, I look back at the list and cringe at how few of these have been met over the years. I can see where she's going with this, and it's not gonna be pretty.

"Alright, Dan. You start. Read out your list," Theresa says with an encouraging smile.

"Okay. One: support my career. Two: uh, sex." He glances at Theresa, but she gives him a nod to continue. "Three: to feel secure in our relationship. That's all I have. I'm a pretty simple guy." He shrugs and clears his throat.

"Completely fine. Now, how many of those would you say Jessie was meeting before the separation?"

"Before spring training, I would have said all of them. Sometimes, I may not have felt one hundred percent supported in my career, especially with her pushing for me to retire. But yeah, for the most part, she was meeting all of them."

She gives him a nod and turns her gaze to me. "Jessie, go ahead and share your list."

I clear my throat and read my paper. "One: having a say on big life decisions and feeling like a full partner. Two: feeling supported in my business. Three: being able to trust he'll do what he says. Four: quality time where he feels present and is actively paying attention. And five: physical intimacy."

I put my list down on my lap, and I can see Dan studying me out of the corner of my eye. The dread starts in my chest as I wait for Theresa to ask her next question.

"And how many of those needs was Dan meeting?"

I take a deep breath and blow it out. I risk a glance at Dan, who has his forehead furrowed and a frown on his face.

"Just number five."

"So physical intimacy was the only need being met," Theresa clarifies.

"Um, yes, there were times when some others were fine. Especially early in our marriage, but over the last few years, not as much."

Theresa lets a moment of silence hang over us.

"Dan, you look upset. Tell us what you're feeling."

"I guess stunned. I had no idea she felt this way. Why didn't you say something? Years, Jessie? You've been feeling this way for years and never said anything?"

"I used to, especially before California. But you'd just make promises to work on it without changing anything, so I slowly stopped saying anything." I shrug with tears filling my eyes.

Dan looks shocked and sad. I knew this would be hard, and we've barely even scratched the surface. Dan clears his throat and huffs. "I'd like to add a number four to my list. Not having secrets between us. I didn't think we had any before all of this, but it's clear she's been keeping all kinds of fucking secrets from me."

"Okay. We're just about out of time for today, and this sounds like something we'll need more time to dig into. So, here's what we're going to do. This week, I'd like you both to think about ways you could meet the needs of the other and think about if those are things you would be willing to commit to doing going forward."

I nod, but I can't help thinking that even if Dan were to commit to working on things, how could I ever trust that he means it? He can tell me he wants to do better a million times, but I've had enough false promises from him to last a lifetime. Can I really keep giving him more chances to break my heart?

A couple of weeks later, we're back in Theresa's office, and shit is hitting the fan. We spent the last two weeks discussing the history of our relationship. She asked me to point out where I thought things went downhill, and I realized it was hard to pinpoint. It's been such a snowball of little things.

Dan has gotten grumpier with each week of counseling. He's not enjoying hearing about the last few years from my perspective, and he looks like he's about to snap.

"I'd like to circle back to something Dan said in our first session about Jessie keeping secrets. Your remark felt very pointed, Dan. Do you want to elaborate?"

Oh shit. I knew the trust fund was going to come back to bite me in the ass.

"She hid a trust fund from me," he grumbles.

"It was more of a lack of a trust fund," I murmur. Theresa gestures for me to continue, so I explain further. "My parents didn't want me to get married straight out of college. They really only care about money and didn't think Dan was good enough because he didn't come from money. He was still in the minors, so he wasn't making the big pro baller salary yet, and my parents had no faith he ever would. I was supposed to get access to my trust fund after I graduated from college, but they threatened to change the terms if I got married. I did it anyway and didn't get access to my trust fund until I turned thirty. I have not touched it; I didn't want their money and have barely spoken to them in years. I'll use it if I need to for supporting my child, as a last resort, but otherwise, I don't want anything from them."

"You won't need to use it for my kid," Dan practically growls at me.

Theresa keeps us moving past Dan's declaration. "Why did you decide not to share this information with Dan?"

"He put so much pressure on himself about money. He knew I grew up wealthy and was so focused on it. I didn't want to add any stress." I bite my lip, hoping they'll let it drop there.

"Is that all?"

Damn, she's good.

"I was afraid he'd call things off. That he'd send me back to my parents for my own good."

"I wouldn't have," Dan interjects.

"You don't know that!" I raise my voice, losing all sense of the little bit of calm I'd been holding onto. "You were so stressed about giving me the life you thought I should have. Big house, cars, expensive clothes. I was afraid that if you found out what I was giving up to be with you, you'd send me packing."

"I did give you all of those things. We have the dream house, your closet is full, and you drive a new car. I gave you everything your parents could."

"Those things were never important to me, though!" I shout. "I wanted what only you could give me. What they never did. Your love. Your attention. Your respect. But those are the things you couldn't seem to provide. I wanted a partnership where I felt like I mattered. I never really mattered to my parents unless I was doing exactly what they wanted me to do. You constantly cut me out of decisions and never seemed to have any spare attention for the things that interested me. You were only concerned with baseball and pushing for a baby you wouldn't even be around to help with. After a while, it felt like living in my parents' house with the pressure to follow their plans, my feelings be damned. Why the fuck would I stay?"

My words ring out, and a tense silence fills the air as I try to mop up the tears flowing down my cheeks. Dan is holding his face in his hands, and his shoulders are shaking. I'm not sure I've ever seen Dan cry like this. The occasional glassy eyes, sure, but full-on crying?

I hate this. I hate that my honesty is hurting him. I hate that we got to this point.

"Okay. Let's shift focus a bit. For the last few weeks, we've spent time with both of you detailing some areas where your marriage may have struggled, so now we're going to spend some time focusing on the good. You're going to go back and forth and tell each other your favorite things about your relationship. Things you appreciate about each other. Who wants to start?"

Dan clears his throat and sniffles a bit. "I'll go first. I appreciate how you've made every place we've lived feel homey. Even the shitty little apartment in Pennsylvania, when we had hardly any money; you made it comfortable."

"I appreciate how you always made time to talk to me when you were on the road. It made me feel close to you," I say softly with a sad smile.

"I appreciate how you've always taken care of me. Whether I'm injured or sick, even from miles away, you'd find ways to make sure I had what I needed."

"I appreciate how you've always made me feel sexy. We've been together for so long, and I never felt like the attraction between us faded or got boring."

Our eyes lock and, for just a moment, heat rises between us. Our physical chemistry has never been the problem, and the second-trimester hormones are kicking in. If we were alone right now, we'd be headed for some crazy makeup sex.

Theresa clears her throat to remind us we are most definitely not alone, and it snaps us both out of the lusty haze. We both turn on the sofa to look back at her.

"How did this exercise feel?" she asks with a polite smile, ignoring the fact that we were seconds away from making out on her therapy couch.

"Good. It felt good," Dan mumbles, and I nod my agreement, not quite ready to find my voice.

"Good. We'll do that exercise every time we meet. I think it feels like a good way to end our sessions, so we're done for today."

We both thank her and shuffle out to the lobby. When we hit the parking lot, we turn toward each other with an awkward smile before we both burst into laughter.

"Well, that was fucking intense," Dan says after our laughter has calmed down. He pulls at the back of his neck and gives me a sheepish smile.

"Which part? The screaming at each other or the almost jumping each other in front of our therapist?"

He huffs a laugh. "Both."

I swallow hard and say the one thing I meant to say earlier. "I'm sorry I didn't tell you about the trust fund. I always meant to. I thought if we could get to a stronger place financially, then it wouldn't add pressure. Then, I low-key forgot about it for a while. When I realized we were coming up on my having access to it, things were already strained, and I didn't want to make everything worse."

He nods his head and grimaces. "I'm sorry you didn't think you could share everything with me."

We stand awkwardly side by side. Counseling has brought so much into the light, and we've hashed out so many issues, but I don't know where we go from here. How do I move on from the hurt and disappointment? How can we rebuild this, knowing how easily it can crumble back down? How do I learn to trust him again?

A couple of months ago, I was so sure I was done, but now I don't think I could walk away knowing I didn't do everything I could to make it work. Not just for me and Dan, but for our baby. If there's a chance we can fix this mess and be a happy family together, I have to try.

From the Anniversary Journal of: Dan & Jessie Chase

Year Eight

Hers:

This was probably our roughest year of our marriage yet. Even more tense than California. On the positive side, my business is finally in a good position. I have two wonderful employees who help me run the show, and we're really thriving. I've tried to put more focus on my business because everything else has been a shitshow. Work is my happy place.

The tension has ramped up between me and Dan. All his hints about retirement meant nothing last year, which, honestly, I had kind of suspected. He signed another one-year contract at the beginning of the season. Didn't even discuss it with me, as if his choices don't affect me. If he wasn't ready to retire, it's fine. He's the one who's been leading the conversation about retiring, not me. I understand it will be hard for him to walk away from baseball. I'm mostly just hurt he left me out of the decision-making. He said all these things about retiring, only to go back on it without a single word.

If it wasn't bad enough, he's gotten really pushy about the baby thing. I don't know why he doesn't understand. I know there are plenty of athletes' wives who have no problems growing their families, but this is just how I feel. That's great for them, but I want Dan to be involved. It's like he wants the status of being a dad without doing any of the work.

I guess it makes sense since he's got the title of husband without ever being emotionally present with me. Other than a joint bank account and regular sex, it's like we don't share anything during the season. He doesn't know what's going on with my business, doesn't know what projects I want to do with the house, and doesn't know what's going on with my friends.

For people who talk to each other every day, sometimes we feel like strangers. If I stopped answering my phone, would he even notice? If I didn't talk to him when he's at home, would he care? I'm not so sure.

I'm trying not to give up hope that we can turn things around between us. He's promised me this will be his last year, and he'll retire at the end of the season. I want to believe him, but I don't think it's what he really wants. He swears he's ready. I have to hold on to the hope that he'll keep his word, for once, and we'll be able to start the next phase of our life in year nine!

XO, Jessie

His:

Chapter Fourteen

Dan

AFTER THE EMOTIONAL ROLLER coaster of a counseling appointment this afternoon, I asked Bailey to come over and hang out. A guys' night felt like a good way to decompress after all the bombs Jessie dropped on me in therapy. I've been clinging to my pride, my righteous anger about her being the one who bailed, but after today... I'm not so sure I have a right to be pissed.

Bailey's off tonight since the Flash have a home game tomorrow afternoon. I got lucky that Leena has plans with Jessie and Annie tonight. He doesn't like to spend his limited nights off away from her, which I get. Bailey's got his priorities in the right order, but I'm still glad the girls have their own plans for the night.

He and his brother, Griffin, who just moved to town last week, show up with a couple of pizzas and a twelve-pack of beer right around dinnertime. Eric joins shortly after him; Annie also left him alone for the night. I'm ready for some bro time. Watching some baseball and shooting the shit with my friends will help shake the emotions of this afternoon.

We're hanging out in my living room watching the Cincinnati vs. Charlotte game when Bailey clears his throat and asks, "Dan, how's couples' counseling going?"

I let out a groan. "Dude. I wanted to have a bro night so I could stop focusing on my fucked-up relationship. I don't need to hash this all out with you assholes."

He chuckles as he takes a sip of his beer. He's not pitching tomorrow, but it's still likely the only one he'll have. When he's pitching, he doesn't drink at all the night before. I crack open my second one and take a big gulp before answering his question. "It's fucking intense."

"What do you mean?" Eric asks, eyebrows raised in question. I debate keeping my shit to myself. I can assume Bailey and Eric will fill in their better halves on this conversation when they get home. But honestly, I need a sounding board to discuss counseling other than my mother.

"Well, one minute we were screaming at each other and crying, and then not even a few minutes later we were inches away from fucking each other on our therapist's couch." I let out a humorless laugh. "Kind of a mind-fuck."

"It's a good sign the sexual tension is still there," Griffin chimes in. I don't know him well, but he seems like a good dude. "By the time my ex-wife and I made it to couples counseling, any spark we had was already dead."

"Fuck, that sucks. So you did counseling, but still ended up divorced?"

Griffin nods his head and shrugs a bit. I feel bad grilling him for info, but I'm not gonna turn down getting perspective from someone who's been where I am. He doesn't look upset at my prying into his business.

"Yeah, it was our last-ditch attempt to salvage things. I fought her on the divorce longer than I should have. She was right; our relationship had run its course. I just hated the idea of giving up." He shrugs again.

I frown down at my beer bottle. Is that where Jessie and I are? Has our relationship run its course, and I'm too stubborn to admit it?

"How did you know it had run its course?" I ask quietly. Fuck, I barely know this guy, and here I am interrogating him about his failed marriage, but I need answers.

"For one, it had been years since we had had sex."

"Years?" Bailey barks out. "Fuck man. Should have been a red flag right there."

"It was. We didn't connect like we did in the early days. Although looking back, even in our early days, we were never hot and heavy. Between our careers and two kids, we didn't make time for each other. I think she may have had something with a coworker at one point, too. I don't think she full-on cheated, but she was checked out of our relationship. Now we can both move on without feeling guilty."

"I'm guessing you've been moving on a whole bunch in those weekends without the kids," Bailey jeers at his brother. Griffin's cheeks go pink, and he shakes his head as he gulps his beer.

"Not as much as you'd think," he grumbles. "There have been a few, um, wild nights out, especially right after the divorce was finalized, but now I mostly sit in my empty house, missing my kids. I'll tell you one thing: the split custody thing sucks ass."

My heart squeezes. If Jessie and I can't work things out, I'm looking at a long road of trading time with our kid. At the beginning, the baby will need to be with Jess, so who knows when I'll see them. For all my carrying on about not needing to be there every second, I'm hating the idea of missing a single second of my baby's life. I swallow down another gulp of beer, trying to push down the lump in my throat.

"Do you think you guys will work it out?" Eric asks me quietly. I'm sure he's gotten Jessie's side of things through Annie, and his question gives me a little hope she hasn't written me off completely yet.

"I hope so. I want to." I take another long drink of my beer to help me gather my thoughts. "I'm so pissed she kept so much from me. She's been unhappy for years and never said a thing. I feel blindsided, but also so fucking guilty I didn't notice. How could I not fucking notice?"

"Look, man, I won't say you were blameless; you made some shitty decisions, but if she didn't communicate that there was a problem, it's on her. You're not a mind reader," Bailey says.

"He's right. It takes two people to ruin a relationship, but now you know, you can do whatever you can to fix it. If it's what you want, of course," Griffin chimes in.

"It is. I'll do whatever it takes to win Jessie back," I say with a fervor that surprises me. I've been so focused on the things she kept from me and the fact that she was willing to walk away, but it's time to focus on what I can do to win her over. I'm not ready to call it quits on our marriage.

It's time I proved it to her.

"Dan, will you come in here a second?" my mom's voice rings out from down the hall. She's been on a dusting kick for the last few days. I think she's going a bit stir crazy being here with me now that I don't need as much help. I'm honestly surprised she's still here and hasn't gone back to Charlotte yet.

I walk into the home office to find her trying to move the desk away from the wall. Jessie set up this room so she could run her business from home, so it's set up like a real executive office, including the huge corner desk with a tall bookshelf attached. Mom's wedged against the wall, pushing with all her strength, but she's not making much progress.

"Mom, what are you doing?" I huff out a laugh as I use my good arm to slide the desk with ease. Mom shoots me a dirty look before crouching down to grab whatever she was trying to get behind the desk.

"Oh, I was dusting in here and accidentally knocked some books back behind the desk. I thought I could get them out, but the desk is too close to the wall and too heavy for me." She stands up from her crouched position with several notebooks in her hands. I slide the desk back against the wall as she plops into the desk chair to catch her breath. She tosses the books onto the desk and blows out a breath. "Thanks, bud."

After a momentary breather, she's back on her feet, rearranging the notebooks back into their places. My eyes are drawn to the assortment of framed photos Jessie has on the desk in here. So many pictures of the two of us, grinning at the camera or gazing at each other. We looked so happy. I study Jessie in the photos as if I could pinpoint where she stopped being happy.

"I remember this! I gave you guys this journal at your wedding!" Mom exclaims, holding up a small white book.

I chuckle as I remember the journal Mom's holding. "Yeah, Jessie was so excited. She begged me to write in it the day after our wedding. I don't think we ever wrote in it again after that, though."

Mom opens the small journal and flips through it before her gaze pops up to meet mine. "You may not have written in it, but it looks like Jessie did."

"What?"

"Look, she's written in it every year."

I grab the tiny notebook and turn the pages, and sure enough, each year has an entry in the "hers" section of the page. The blank "his" sections make me queasy with guilt. Direct evidence of my neglect in black and white.

"You said the other day you wished you could go back and figure out when things started going downhill," Mom murmurs, squeezing my forearm. "Here's your chance. Maybe this little journal will give you some insights Jessie kept to herself."

I nod and leave Mom to her dusting, taking the white notebook with me. I close myself in my bedroom, ready to figure out where things went wrong in my marriage.

The journal is funny at first. Jessie's early entries are light and bubbly, just how I remember her. She decided early on to use the journal to vent since I wouldn't write in it. I get a massive jolt of guilt seeing how I blew her off on our first anniversary. I thought the journal was dumb and a waste of time. What a dick move.

As the years go on, I can feel Jessie's tone change. She sounds worn down. Even on paper, some of her upbeat sentences fall flat. Like she's putting on a brave face but can't quite keep the truth out of her words. The things that started as minor complaints have become huge grievances. They became evidence of my not caring about her interests. *Fuck.*

I cringe through the California years. I knew she didn't love it there, but I definitely didn't know how bad it was for her. I had no idea she felt this way about the other WAGs. I remember her complaining, but I shrugged her off. Made excuses about needing time to get comfortable.

When I get to year eight, my stomach is in knots. She was so upset, so hurt, and I didn't know a thing about it. Dread creeps over me as I flip to year nine.

Year Nine

Hers:

Not sure why I'm even bothering to update this thing anymore. Guess who didn't retire this year after he PROMISED me he would? Guess who didn't even consult me when he made that choice? Guess who keeps pushing and pushing for me to get pregnant despite knowing exactly how I feel about it?

He promised again that this is the last year, but at this point, I don't even know how to trust him. He's promised he'll try to be more present; he promised me he'd help me with the projects I have saved; he promised a lot of things he clearly has no intention of doing. Why would I believe anything he says at this point?

Do I even want a baby? My business is finally in a good spot. Another local event planner, Charlie, came to work for me this year. We have two assistants who float between our events. We're doing amazing. I'd have to rearrange everything to take care of a newborn, even if Dan retires. Is it worth it to have a baby with a man I'm not sure I can trust to make me—us—a priority? If he really retires this year, it will show me he's ready, but we'll see. I'm certainly not holding my breath. I'd probably suffocate...

I don't really know where to go from here, and at this point, I'm so tired. Tired of fighting for an ounce of his attention. Tired of hoping we'll get back to how we were at the beginning of our relationship. Tired of waiting for him to see me again.

I love Dan so much, and the idea of leaving him sends literal spikes of pain through my heart. I never thought I'd even think of divorce as an option, and the thought still makes me sick to my stomach. But I'm not sure how much more I can take of him only caring about his own needs...

XO, Jessie

His:

Fuck.

Our anniversary is in July. She was already thinking of leaving me when she wrote this last summer. She didn't trust me. Jessie was already at the end of her rope, and this was months before she pulled the trigger and left. A decision years in the making. My flippant choice to run off to spring training was the last straw.

I lower my head into my hands, and a broken sob leaves my body. I've never been much of a crier, but fuck, it feels like my heart's shattering. No wonder she wants to be done with me. She's been slowly breaking down for years, and I was too self-absorbed to see it. I remember these fights. Instead of taking them seriously, I blew her off, assuming she'd get over it.

But she wasn't getting over it; she was powering through until my bullshit was just too much for her to handle anymore.

I don't even deserve her after everything I put her through.

There's a soft knock on my bedroom door, and Mom's voice calls my name through the door. I do my best to mop up my snotty, tear-soaked face before calling out for her to come in. She takes one look at my face and climbs onto my bed with me, wrapping me in a hug that makes me feel like a little kid again. I'm pretty sure I was a kid the last time I cried like this.

"Oh, honey. I'm guessing the journal was a tough read."

I bark out a humorless laugh. "You could say that."

"Did it help you understand Jessie a little better?" she asks softly.

I draw a deep, stuttering breath and nod my head. "Yeah, it did. But it also makes me think we can't fix this. She gave me so many chances, and I put myself first over and over again. Lied and made promises I never intended to keep. I wouldn't trust me either."

"Everyone makes mistakes. The important thing is learning from them." She runs her hand through my hair, just like she did when I was little and needed soothing.

"I fucked this all up. I don't know how to fix it," I croak out.

"You fix it by being honest with her. By apologizing, acknowledging where you went wrong, and committing to not making those same mistakes again. Then, you do it. Only make promises you can keep. You'll have to prove she can trust you to do what you say you'll do."

I nod my head and pick up the journal from where I dropped it in my distress.

"The journal gives you a head start. At least you know where you went wrong."

"You're right. I have to at least try."

She rubs my back for a long minute before standing up and checking her watch.

"Dinner will be done in a little while. You come on down when you're ready."

I nod and pick up the journal again. I read through it a few more times, internalizing more things about where I went wrong. Things I could have noticed. Things I could have appreciated. I took this woman for granted in more ways than I can count.

It ends now. I wanted to know where I went wrong, and I fucking got a clear guide of all my mistakes. Now I'm going to do everything in my power to prove to Jessie I won't make the same mistakes again.

I was so focused on my career, I let everything else fall apart. Instead of building up and cherishing the life that would be left after I was done playing, I neglected it and let it fall apart. Baseball was my dream job, but it was always going to be temporary. Jessie and I were supposed to be forever. I'm not ready to give up on forever. I'm going to win back my wife, and I'm going to be the best damn husband and father.

I've got a new dream job now.

Chapter Fifteen

Jessie

WE'RE QUIET AS WE sit in Theresa's waiting room the week after our big counseling blow-up. Dan seems sad today, and as angry as I am at him, I don't like it. I'm a chatty person by nature, so this tense silence between us makes me choose small talk over stewing in my anxiety.

"So, you got the cast off?" I ask unnecessarily.

He nods and shoots me a careful smile. "Yep, it's all healed up. I'm supposed to keep doing PT with Eric for a while, but otherwise, I can fully use my arm again. It was kind of weird driving myself here today."

I chuckle and shoot him a timid smile back. "Is your mom still in town?"

"She's driving back down tomorrow, but she said she'd be back soon. She's planning on moving up here. She even had a couple of job interviews while she was here."

"She mentioned moving to me the last time we talked. It'll be nice to have a grandparent close for the munchkin." I smile more fully at Dan now. A spark of excitement shines in his eyes at the mention of the baby.

Theresa pops out into the waiting room to usher us in. We take our usual seats, and she smiles at us. "How are we doing this week? Dan, I see you have two arms again. Has to feel good." We all chuckle at her joke.

"It does. I was ready to get the stupid, itchy cast off, that's for sure."

"And Jessie, how are you feeling? How many weeks now?"

"Seventeen weeks, right?" he interjects. My eyebrows shoot up in shock at him knowing what week we're on. He sees my surprise and cringes. "I downloaded an app on my phone to keep track of the weeks."

"You did?" I ask, completely floored that he cared enough to download an app. I don't think Dan will be a bad dad, but I also didn't think he'd be so invested in the pregnancy process. Just like how I never doubted Dan loved me, but putting in effort to show it was never his forte.

"Yeah. I needed to stay connected to you guys while we're not living together."

I don't respond. He makes our living arrangement sound temporary. I'm not sure what's changed, but he's acting differently since last week. It's like all the frustrated anger that's colored all our interactions for the last couple of months has disintegrated, and I don't know why.

"Jessie, you seem surprised. What's going through your head?" Theresa interjects.

"Um, I guess I'm just a little confused."

"Why?"

I furrow my brow, trying to find the right words. "It feels out of character. Like, I know Dan wants to be a part of this baby's life, but I wouldn't have expected him to be this invested before the baby's actually here."

"Dan, any response? How does it make you feel to hear these things from Jessie?" Theresa asks kindly.

I see his jaw clench, and I get ready for him to be pissed and defensive. I study my hands, waiting to hear his excuses.

"It hurts to hear, but I can't say she's wrong." My head snaps up to look at him, and he winces before he continues. "I've realized I've taken a lot for granted over the years. I focused on myself and baseball while Jess took care of everything else. I can see why she'd expect nothing from me."

My jaw drops as I stare at the alien currently inhabiting my husband's body. It's the only explanation for this total one-eighty I can think of.

"Who are you and what have you done with Dan?" I blurt out.

He huffs a laugh and turns to face me more. "I'm just seeing things from your side. Seeing the mistakes I made that brought us to this."

I'm stunned. I never thought we'd get to the point where he understood. I don't know where we go from here. Tears stream down my face at hearing the last few years of frustration validated by him.

"Jessie, I can see you're having a lot of feelings about what Dan is saying. Do you want to share some of how you're feeling?"

She shoves the tissue box on the coffee table closer to me, and I gratefully grab a few of them to mop up the tears I can't seem to stop.

"I think I'm mostly relieved. It felt like he'd never see my side of things and never understand why I was ready to walk away." I swallow hard. "I'm also worried. I don't know where we go from here. Like, I appreciate he seems to understand where I'm coming from, but I don't know if I can trust he'd make any changes."

I can see the hurt flicker through Dan's eyes, but he looks chagrined instead of mad.

"I get it. I've done nothing but bullshit you for years. For what it's worth, Jessie Baby, I'm really sorry. I had my head so far up my own ass, I never really stopped to think about how my choices were affecting you.

I should have retired when I said I would; I just wasn't ready to let go of baseball."

"You could have told me. I was never pissed about your wanting to play longer. It was how you would say one thing and do another without so much as a conversation. I only ever wanted to be your partner."

I'm shocked all over again to see tears slide down Dan's cheek. This whole counseling session has felt like a total mind-fuck. Theresa slides the tissue box over to Dan, and he takes one to wipe across his face.

"Alright, this feels like fantastic progress in furthering your communication. Now we need to move toward building some trust between the two of you. Do you have any ideas about how?"

I swallow hard. How can I learn to trust him again? I'm about to tell her I don't know when Dan speaks up, "What if we started dating? Like a reset on our relationship?"

"So, like, add in date nights?"

"No, more than that. More like starting at the beginning, doing all the things people in new relationships do to get to know each other. Texting, phone calls, dates." He looks nervous, like I might shoot down an idea he is clearly excited about trying.

I mull it over and glance at Theresa, who is already nodding. She obviously approves of this plan.

"It's not like we can just hit reset on the last thirteen years and everything we've been through, though," I say cautiously.

Theresa pipes up, "Jessie, you're right. You can't reset the past, and there will definitely still be work you both need to do to move beyond it. But I believe what Dan's suggesting is more about meeting each other as you are now, and spending time getting to know who you've each become. People change drastically from their early twenties to their early thirties. You've both developed into different people than you were when you first met. Going through the motions of starting a 'new' relationship will help you both determine if you're still compatible and if you'd rather continue in your marriage or if you're better off co-parenting as friends."

Dan swallows hard. He very clearly doesn't love the idea that this could still lead us to end things once and for all. I can see the doubt flicker through his expression before he shakes it away and meets my gaze.

"I think we should do this, Jessie. Give us a chance to get to know each other again without the baggage of the mistakes I've made." His eyes are pleading, and the sincerity blazing from them finally cracks the armor I've built around my heart these last few months.

"Okay. We'll try it," I say softly.

"Thank you," he murmurs back. We hold each other's eyes for a long moment before Theresa responds.

"Good. I think this will be good. Do your best not to dig into past struggles when you're in dating mode. You can save some of those conversations for when you're here. Obviously, do what comes naturally, but I think it will benefit you to think of this as a new relationship you're both entering. I look forward to hearing about it at our next session."

I nod and thank Theresa before making my way out to my car in a worried daze. Dan stays behind to ask her another question, but I keep moving, lost in my thoughts. Can I really put aside everything that's consumed our marriage over the last few months? The last few years, really.

"Hey, Jessie, wait up!" I hear Dan call out behind me as I reach the sunny parking lot. It's a perfect mid-May day with the temperatures in the upper seventies, and the bright blue skies help me shake some of the panic at this dating idea. I turn and wait outside my car for Dan to catch up, which doesn't take long as his muscular legs carry him quickly over to me.

I take a moment to study him as he approaches. He looks good in his khaki shorts and tight black T-shirt, showing off his still clearly-defined muscles. A broken arm has not done much damage to his physique. Fuck, these pregnancy hormones are not my friends as I watch him approach.

"What do you think about Saturday?"

"What about Saturday?"

"For our first date?" He looks nervous. Is he worried I'll change my mind?

"What do you want to do?" I ask cautiously. Most of our date nights over the last few years comprised of dinner in a random restaurant, usually one with a TV so he could still watch whatever baseball games were on, then we'd go home. Occasionally, they'd include a movie, but even those instances were pretty rare in the last couple of years.

"I have an idea, but I'd rather it be a surprise. Can I call you with the details?"

I narrow my eyes at him, trying to figure out what he's up to. He shoots me a smirk that makes heat pool in my belly, and I decide it's time to get the fuck out of here before the pregnancy hormones make me do something I don't want to do.

"Yeah, that's fine. Just text me."

He nods and reaches past me to open my car door for me. He leans in and presses a chaste kiss on my cheek as he murmurs, "I'll see you Saturday."

I mumble a reply, too flustered to say anything real. How is this man, whom I've been with for well over a decade, giving me butterflies right now? I plop into my seat and get the car moving as quickly as I can, offering Dan a small wave as I drive away.

What the fuck did I just agree to?

On Saturday afternoon, I pop down to the bar about an hour before Dan is supposed to pick me up. What I wouldn't give to have some liquid courage before this date, but of course, the bell pepper-sized munchkin I'm carrying around rules it out.

Dan told me to dress casually, so I'm wearing a mint green light cotton dress. It flows over the tiny baby bump that's formed over the last few weeks. I added a pair of comfy Keds sneakers and my sling bag. I double-check the pockets on my dress for lip gloss and my phone before plopping onto a barstool.

Leena and Cass are behind the bar, going over some inventory paperwork, when I sit down. Cass comes over and pours me a Sprite without me having to ask. We've spent a lot more time together over the last few months, with me living upstairs and her working all the time. I'm not sure I'd consider us close, but we're more like friends than we used to be.

"You look nice. Where are you headed?" Leena asks, slightly confused. I haven't gotten around to filling Leena and Annie in on this whole new dating idea yet.

"She's got a date," Cass answers snarkily. She was here when I got back from counseling on Thursday, so she knows my date is with Dan.

Leena's eyes widen. "What? You're dating?"

I roll my eyes at Cass. "I have a date with Dan."

"I still don't understand," Leena says, looking back and forth between me and Cass for an explanation.

"Our therapist thought it might be good for us to spend some time together. Kind of like a reset where we act like this is a new relationship rather than one that's slowly been dying for years."

"Okay, then." Leena eyes me for a long moment. "You're nervous, aren't you?"

I blow out a big breath and throw my hands up. "Yes, but it doesn't make any sense. It's just Dan."

"Are you nervous the date won't go well? Or are you maybe more nervous he'll sweep you off your feet like he did in college and you'll have to forgive him for all the shit that's gone down?"

I pin Leena with a hard stare. I sometimes hate how well she knows me because she just summed up exactly what I'm nervous about. I sip my drink and decide not to answer her.

Leena just laughs and continues, "Do you want to work things out with Dan? Big picture, do you see yourselves together?"

I sigh. "I don't know. Part of me wants it, especially when I picture us with the munchkin. I hate the idea of passing a baby back and forth.

Missing holidays and bedtimes because it's Dad's weekend. But there's also a part of me that's not sure I can move on from the pain of the last few years."

Leena nods. "Well, since you're not sure, you have to give Dan a real chance to prove he can be trusted. If he wants another shot, he can earn it. And you can prove you're willing to share how you're feeling with him. Communication is a two-way street, babes, and you aren't totally blameless in all of this. You kept a lot of things hidden from him."

I clench my jaw and glare at her. This is the problem with lifelong friends. They'll call you on your bullshit. "I really hate it when you're right."

Leena shoots me a cocky grin. "I know!"

"Speak of the devil," Cass murmurs as the door to the bar opens.

I look up to see Dan glancing around the room. When he finds me at the bar, his face lights up with a bright smile, and those butterflies from the other day are back. I can't remember the last time I got the fluttery feeling in my gut looking at Dan, but here we are. He stops next to my stool and leans down to kiss my cheek.

"You look beautiful, Jessie. You ready to go?"

"Hold up a minute. What are your intentions with our Jessie, strange man?" Leena asks in a mock-serious tone.

I roll my eyes, and Dan laughs. "I promise not to keep her out too late, ma'am."

"Oh, ew, don't you 'ma'am' me!" Leena whines.

We all laugh at her antics as Dan helps me down from my barstool. His eyes travel the length of my body, pausing on my bump. "Fuck, baby, you're starting to show. Look at this little bump."

He reaches and places both hands on the swell of my belly, and I freeze at the touch. Not because I'm uncomfortable, but because this feels so natural. It's exactly how it should be, and the awe on his face as he holds the tiny evidence of his child in his hands makes all of my emotions rise to the surface.

He looks up into my eyes, and I see the panic flicker through his eyes. "Shit, sorry." He tries to pull back, but I hold on to his hands to keep him there.

"It's okay," I murmur. We stand still, studying each other's eyes until Leena clears her throat, reminding us we're not having this tender moment alone. Dan takes a step back and clears his throat.

"You ready?"

I smile up at him, my nerves for this date having melted away after whatever just passed between us. "Let's go!"

I shoot Leena and Cass a wave and follow Dan out into the May sunshine.

Chapter Sixteen
Dan

"OH MY GOSH, YOU didn't!" Jessie exclaims as she sees the miniature golf course come into view. I don't say anything in response, but I shoot her a smile as I pull into a parking spot. "I don't think we've mini-golfed since Charlotte!"

I cringe at the thought, but she's right. On our very first date, I took her to a miniature golf course a few miles away from campus, and it was something we did often until a few years ago. It's always been our thing, but we're way overdue for a mini-golf date. Another thing I stopped making time for while I put all of my energy into my career and none into my marriage. *Shit.* Should I have even brought us here?

One look at Jessie's big, bright smile eases some of my fears. She looks happy to be here, practically bouncing in her seat.

"You ready to get your ass beat, Chase?" Jessie teases. On our first date, I learned just how competitive my girl was.

"You're on, Jessie Baby!"

As we walk over to the little building to rent clubs, I take a risk and grab Jessie's hand. I did the same thing on our first date, but it feels much riskier now. Back then, we had already explored our instant chemistry with a wild make-out session in the basement of the baseball off-campus party house. The date was more about moving us from hookup to official relationship status. There's way more at stake now.

She tenses for just a second when our hands meet, then relaxes and smiles shyly at me. I'm sure she's remembering our first date just as much as I do. We get our supplies and start the course. Jessie usually schools my ass at mini golf, but she's struggling today with her shots going wild and hitting all the obstacles just wrong.

"Goddammit!" she yells, earning us dirty looks from a family a few holes away from us. I shoot them an apologetic glance before moving to stand behind Jessie.

Close enough to murmur in her ear, "You're gonna get us kicked out of here, baby."

She makes a frustrated half-laugh, half growl sort of noise. "This is all your fault!"

"What? How is it *my* fault?"

"You knocked me up! Completely ruined my center of gravity, and now I suck at mini golf." She runs a hand through her blonde waves in frustration. She stills and meets my eyes for a moment before throwing her head back and laughing at the silliness of it all. I'm laughing so hard I have tears running out of the corners of my eyes. I can't remember the last time we laughed together like this, and it makes my stomach clench.

We play through the course, an undercurrent of mirth between us. Neither of us is very good, and it makes it even more fun. We turn our clubs back in and get back in the car.

"I didn't make a definite plan for dinner since I wasn't sure what the munchkin would want? What's she thinking?"

"She? You think it's a she?"

"I'm happy either way, but my gut feeling is a girl." I shrug at her. I don't tell her I'm hoping it's a girl. I can't get the vision of a tiny version of Jessie out of my head.

"Do you want to find out?" Jessie asks casually.

"I think I do, do you?"

"Yeah, I don't want to wait."

"Perfect. So, just a couple of weeks until we find out." I reach over and squeeze her hand on the center console. "Now, what does baby want for dinner?"

"Hmm, tacos?" She asks, her eyes lighting up at the thought.

"Real tacos, or Taco Bell?"

"Let's go to Local Cantina so you can get a margarita and I can smell it."

"Smell it?" I ask, confused.

"I can't drink it, so I just want to smell it. Get my fix until this baby comes."

"Why don't you just get a virgin one?" I ask with a chuckle as I get the car moving in the direction of the restaurant.

"It's not the same. I need to smell the tequila."

"Okay, baby. We'll get you a sniffing marg and some tacos."

"Thank you." She nods and looks out the window, but I can see the smile still on her face. God, how did I ever go so long without making her smile like this? One thing's for sure, I'll spend the rest of my life making up for the last several years if she'll let me.

The bar is busy when we get back to drop Jessie off, but I don't see anyone I recognize. Even Cass must have the night off, because their other bartender, Alaina, is behind the bar. Jessie gives her a small wave and walks behind the bar to the back kitchen area, where the stairs to the Songbird apartment are. I follow along behind her, determined to walk her all the way to the door.

She unlocks the door and steps through, but I pause in the doorway. I glance around the single-room apartment. I see instantly how Jessie took the time to decorate the small apartment, and the fact hits me like a slap to the face.

When she moved in here, she made herself at home. She was planning to stay here for a while. The sight of her apartment is driving home the fact that she actually left me. She asked for a divorce. She was ready to walk away because I had my head up my ass and took her for granted.

She must sense the change in my mood because she approaches me slowly. "You okay?"

I blow out a breath. "This place. You look so settled here. It just hit me, you really left and planned to stay gone."

She winces and squeezes my forearm. "I'm sorry. You know how I am with decorating, and I was sad, so it gave me something to focus on and—"

I pull her into my arms to stop her nervous babbling, "Don't apologize, baby. It's my fault. It just hit me how serious you've been. I guess I was still a little bit in denial."

"It's not all your fault," she murmurs into my chest, wrapping her arms around my waist. "It took both of us to get to this point. I could have spoken up more. Made it clear when things weren't working for me."

She leans back, looking up into my eyes. She gives me a soft, sad smile, and I can't resist lowering my mouth to hers. It's been months since I've kissed my wife, and I never want to go so long ever again.

She pushes up on her toes to deepen the kiss, and I run my hands through her hair, holding her in place as I slant my mouth over hers. Her arms are wrapped around my neck, pulling me down to her. She presses her body into mine and lets out a soft moan. I instantly pull back, knowing if we keep this up, we'll end up in the bed in the corner.

"What are you doing?" she asks as I pull away from her.

"We should take things slow." I rest my forehead on hers and do my best to lower my heart rate.

She groans, "We never took it slow when we were first dating." She shoots me a wicked smile that makes my cock jump in my pants.

"Jessie Baby, I don't think I've ever wanted you more than I do right now, but we both know there are things that need to be worked out between us before we jump back into bed."

She lets out a big sigh and rests her head on my chest, wrapping her arms around my waist. "I know you're right. My pregnancy horniness hates it, but you're right."

I laugh. Hopefully, soon we can take advantage of those hormones, but for now, I know this is the right choice. I need her to trust me again before we complicate things with sex. I drop one last quick kiss on her lips before turning to the door.

"I'll text you later, baby."

She smiles at me and nods, and I get the hell out of there before my dick tries to change my mind. Tonight went so well. I'm finally feeling a shred of hope that we can actually fix what's broken in our marriage. I can't afford to do anything to trip us up.

I'm winning my wife back, if it's the last thing I do.

Early the next morning, I'm slicing open a box of flooring panels when the doorbell rings. I wipe my dusty hands on my paint-splattered jeans and head for the door. Bailey and Griffin are waiting on the porch with a tray of coffees from the Songbird, a couple of six packs, and any power tools they own.

"Hey guys, thanks for coming to help me."

"No problem, man." Bailey pats me on my good shoulder as he moves toward the kitchen to put the beer in the fridge for later in the day. "What all do we need to get done?"

"I need help moving the furniture out of the spare bedroom upstairs. I can prep it and paint it myself, but with my bum shoulder, I can't manage the heavy stuff like the mattress. Then the flooring needs to go into the half-bath down here. The plumber and shower installer are all finished, so the flooring is the last piece to finish that project."

"Does Jessie know you're doing any of this?" Griffin asks, pulling one of the coffees out of the tray and handing it to me. I nod my thanks.

"No. I'm keeping it a surprise until at least the indoor projects are done. I still have to put up the frames in the dining room. I painted the wall this week." I gesture to the dining room that has a freshly painted accent wall.

"She's gonna love it. Did you pick the color?" Bailey asks, sipping his coffee.

"Uh, no," I mumble, pulling at the back of my neck as the shame creeps up. "She picked the color a couple of years ago, and I kept putting her off about actually getting it done. I think she eventually gave up. The paint sample was still hanging out in the kitchen junk drawer."

"Better late than never," Griffin says with a shrug and a kind smile. "Where do you want to start?"

"Let's go up and do the furniture. Flooring's a pain in the ass, so let's get the easier job out of the way first."

"Lead the way, man."

We make our way upstairs to the spare bedroom that is closest to the master bedroom. It makes sense that the nursery will be the nearest room to our bedroom, well, my bedroom for now, but hopefully by the time the baby is here, it will be ours again.

"Okay, where are we putting this stuff?" Bailey asks, lifting the edge of the dresser to test its weight.

"The garage. I think we'll donate it all, but I want to make sure Jessie doesn't have any sentimental attachment to any of this."

"Smart."

Between the three of us, we make quick work of the furniture. Once the room is empty, we stand to survey our work.

"What color are you doing this room?" Bailey asks.

"I'll wait for Jessie on this one. And we probably won't decide until we know the gender of the baby. I'm sure Jessie already knows how she wants to decorate either way."

Griffin chuckles as we make our way downstairs to deal with the bathroom flooring. "Yeah, Nessa had Mellie's nursery theme picked before she even got pregnant."

"How are the kids dealing with the move?" Bailey asks. "Last time we talked about it, Mellie still wasn't happy about it."

"Mellie is thirteen. She's not happy about anything these days," Griffin grumbles. "She's pissed about the divorce still, but she's taking most of that out on Nessa, especially since the kids are living with me full time while Nessa gets settled in at the new job."

"Yikes. That's rough," I say sympathetically.

"Comes with the amicable divorce territory, unfortunately. She'll understand someday."

"And you're really just chill with your ex-wife?"

"Oh yeah, Nessa's still one of my best friends. I wasn't on board with splitting up at first, but I'm starting to think we never really had that spark, you know? We were friends who decided to try dating, and it stuck, but we never had a burning passion for each other."

"Jessie and I always had a spark. From the moment we met in college, it was like lightning. Fuck even with us being separated, the spark never went away."

"Yeah, apparently, it's fucking rare," Griffin says, his mood darkening. Bailey and I share a glance, eyebrows raised at Griffin's weird tone shift.

"Something you want to share, Griff?" Bailey asks as he hands Griffin a beer from the fridge.

"Not particularly," Griffin says in a glum voice, shooting a warning glare at Bailey, and I smirk into my beer. "Let's just get that flooring in. Nessa will be bringing the kids back soon." Griffin sets his empty beer bottle down on the counter with a snap and stalks off toward the half bath.

Bailey and I stare at each other, eyebrows raised for a beat before we shrug and chuckle at Griffin's avoidance. Bailey rolls his eyes. "Fine! Keep your secrets!" he yells after Griffin before we both follow to help install the flooring.

When the work is done and the Turner brothers have gone home to their respective houses, I admire the finished bathroom, the accent wall progress, and the empty soon-to-be-nursery. I make mental notes of what I need to finish before Jessie sees it.

This day has turned out to be exactly what I needed. A light day with good friends doing hard physical labor. Labor that will hopefully help me win my wife back. I know we have a ways to go to mend our relationship, but I can't help but feel hopeful. Hopeful that each change I make to the house, each change I make to my perspective, brings her closer to coming home.

Chapter Seventeen

Jessie

It turns out pretending to be in a new relationship with your husband of almost ten years is pretty fun. The connection between us that had all but disappeared is back and feeling stronger than ever. We text all the time, and we've been spending most evenings together doing all the things couples do in the early stages, like going out on dates or staying in and making out while a movie plays in the background. We even went to the last Flash game with our friends to cheer on Bailey and the other guys, Dan's been friends with for years.

We've had a few intense make-out sessions, but Dan's still holding out on me, insisting we take things slow. I'm not gonna lie, it's made everything hotter. I feel eighteen all over again. Between the build-up of tension and the baby hormones fucking with my libido, I'm almost ready to burst.

Tonight, we're doing an open mic date night, and it'll be interesting to see how things feel in a setting so familiar. Even when things were bad, we'd come to open mic and hang out with everyone. It was easy to hide all the ways our marriage was struggling when we could focus on other people.

I give my hair a final fluff as I hear a knock at the door, signaling Dan's arrival with the takeout. I pull the door open for him and lose my breath for just a moment at how gorgeous he looks. He's wearing dark jeans with dressy brown boots. A fitted blue button-down stretches over his muscular frame and brings out the blue tones in his turquoise eyes. His hair's getting a little long on top, and it flops rakishly over his forehead.

"Hey, baby," he murmurs as he leans down to kiss me. "Does the munchkin still want Pad Thai, or am I going back out?"

I chuckle as I move to grab plates out of the cabinet over the sink in my tiny kitchenette. "We're good with Thai. Although I'm still annoyed, I had to drop my spicy level so much. A fucking two! Baby steals everything fun," I grumble as Dan just chuckles and shakes his head.

He's heard my rant about my new and infuriating lack of spice tolerance several times. Luckily, our favorite Thai place lets you order your spiciness on a scale of one to nine. I used to like my Pad Thai with a level six spice, and now I can barely tolerate a two.

We sit at the tiny round table and discuss our days. He fills me in on his PT progress, and we gossip a bit about Eric and Annie, wondering if they'll get engaged soon. I'm hoping they wait until after the baby comes and we get Leena and Bailey's wedding out of the way, but I'll be thrilled for them no matter what.

"How was your meeting today?" Dan asks before shoveling a big bite of noodles into his mouth. I pause for a moment, startled that he remembered. Before all of this, he would never have paid attention enough to know I had a meeting, let alone asked me how it went.

"It was good. We're going to bring on another planner and a third assistant. Charlie and Sam think that between the five of them, they should be good to cover all of my maternity leave."

"Awesome! Wow, five employees. I'm so proud of you, Jessie. You had a vision for your company, and you never let anything, including all the shit my career put you through, get in the way of making it work."

I blush and thank him, stunned at how supportive he's become. Maybe it's stupid of me to believe this is how it will always be, but I can't help it. This new version of Dan makes me feel seen in a way I never did before, even in our early days. A spike of fear climbs my spine, insisting it won't last, but I shake it off, determined to enjoy our night with all our friends.

Open mic night is already underway when we pop out into the bar. I instantly crack up laughing when I find Fred up on stage. He's dressed like a hard rocker from the eighties again and is belting out AC/DC's "You Shook Me All Night Long" to a bar full of people. The crowd always loves it when Fred joins open mic. I'm pretty sure he brainstorms the most ridiculous and wild songs he can perform just to entertain us.

Dan and I join Leena, Annie, and Eric at the bar. Cass looks at me from behind the bar and raises her eyebrows. I smile and nod at her, and she fills a glass with Sprite. As she turns to look at Dan, she drops her smile.

"You want anything?" she says in a grumpy tone. I chuckle under my breath at the grudge she's holding on my behalf.

"I'm good with a Coke," Dan says carefully.

Cass huffs and gets it for him without saying another word.

"Did I do something to piss her off?" he asks, confused.

"Don't worry about her; she likes holding grudges even though I told her we were cool now."

He chuckles, "When did you and Cass become friends?"

I swallow hard before responding, "She was with me when I realized I might be pregnant. She talked me through what I'm pretty sure was a panic attack, drove me to the house, called Leena and Annie for me... We've gotten close these last few months." I shrug, feeling the palpable tension rising between us again. We haven't discussed the time he was away much when we're not in counseling, and I'm worried I just tanked the mood on our night.

Dan reaches out and nudges my chin up so I look at him instead of studying the bar top. "I'm sorry I wasn't here for you. But I'm glad you had your friends looking out for you."

I can see the pain and remorse in his eyes. I offer him a sad smile, and he returns it. I push up on my toes to plant a chaste kiss on his lips.

"Thank you."

The moment passes, and we sip our drinks, listening to Eric tell a funny story about one of his patients. A few minutes later, Bailey and Griffin join us. I met Griffin the other day at Bailey and Leena's house, but this is the first time he's been out with us for open mic night.

Cass comes wandering over but freezes in her tracks when she spots Griffin. "Oh, fuck," she whispers under her breath.

"Cass! Come meet Bailey's brother!" Leena screeches from down the bar, oblivious to Cass's instant reaction to Griffin. I study Cass as she walks toward us woodenly, wondering what's up with her. I glance over at Griffin, and he has a similar stunned expression on his face. There's a story here, I can tell, but knowing Cass, I'll have a hell of a time getting the details out of her. I file it away for another time when I have Cass alone, as I watch their interaction.

"Cass, was it? I'm Griffin." His voice is gruff, almost angry, as he reaches out to shake Cass's hand.

They shake hands, but they hold on a beat too long, the air charged between them. "Nice to meet you," Cass murmurs before clearing her throat and stepping back.

Leena furrows her brow as she looks back and forth between them, clocking the weirdness. Griffin excuses himself to the restroom, and Cass backs away to take drink orders down the bar while we all look at each other with confusion.

"What the fuck?" Annie finally blurts.

Bailey's gaze is on his brother's retreating back. "I'm not sure, but I've never seen him go all gruff. He's usually upbeat and friendly, but I guess he has been kind of cagey lately."

"Cass looked like she'd seen a ghost. There's definitely a story there," I chirp. We all study her for another moment until she shoots a death glare our way. We shrug off the weirdness and go back to discussing what songs our group wants to perform.

Dan nudges me. "Do you want to do a duet?"

My eyebrows shoot up in surprise. He's done duets with me in the past, but I usually had to twist his arm and promise sexual favors to get him to do it. He keeps surprising me.

"Yeah, what did you have in mind?"

"Oh, I'll think of something," he says with a bright smile.

I grin back at him, excited to see what he comes up with.

About an hour later, I'm on stage with a microphone in my hand, and I still have no idea what song Dan picked. I shoot him an anxious look as he joins me on the small stage.

"Are you seriously not gonna tell me?" I ask, low-key panicked. I didn't get a chance to prepare.

"Don't worry, baby. I picked a song you for sure know, and your part doesn't start right away. We'll be fine." He winks and nods at Leena to start the music track.

I instantly recognize "The Next Ten Minutes" from *The Last Five Years,* and I relax. I could sing this musical in my sleep, and he's right: the Cathy part doesn't come in until the second verse.

As I listen to Dan sing the Jamie verse, I start to wonder what made him pick this song. The show is literally the story of how a relationship falls apart. The couple gets divorced in the end. I know it's just a song at open mic night, but it feels like a bad omen.

We make it through the song, but my mind is still stuck in the spiral, thinking about what it all means. Are we going through this whole dating thing to end up divorced, anyway? I've finally gotten to the point where I have hope for our marriage. For so long, it felt like the only way forward was out, but now, I think we could make it work. What if I'm getting my hopes up for nothing?

At the same time, what if we decide to make it work, and all the changes Dan has made evaporate? How do I know if I can trust him to keep up his end of the bargain when it's what got us into this mess in the first place? The questions keep cycling through my brain, making me irritated and sad.

Dan can sense my weird mood, and he keeps shooting me worried looks. So do Leena, Annie, and Cass, but I can't shake it. Even singing "Golden" from *K-Pop Demon Hunters* with Leena and Annie can't quite lift me out of my spiraling worries.

Eventually, Dan asks if I'm ready to head upstairs, and I nod. We say a quick goodnight to our friends, and we head behind the bar. We're both quiet going up the stairs, and I know we have a conversation coming. I need answers to some of the questions flying through my brain.

The door closes behind us, and I can feel Dan's eyes on me as I fill my water bottle at the fridge. I'm avoiding his gaze, trying to decide what I want to say first when he beats me to it.

"Jessie. Can you look at me?" he says in a tortured voice. I clench my jaw and lift my eyes to his. I can see the pain and worry in his gaze, and I'm flooded with guilt for acting so weird tonight. "What's going on?"

"Why did you pick that song?" I ask quietly. He startles, like he wasn't expecting it to be the first thing I said.

"Uh, I looked up romantic Broadway duets and remembered you liked the show," he mumbles and shrugs. "The lyrics seemed nice."

I stare at him for a long moment before throwing my head back and laughing hysterically, relief making me feel crazy. The confusion filling his face only makes me laugh harder before I collapse onto the couch, unable to stay upright. I got so in my head about his song choice meaning something, and he doesn't even remember the story of *The Last Five Years*.

"Oh my God, I'm sorry," I wheeze out between laughs. He comes over to sit next to me on the couch with a wary expression on his face.

"You want to fill me in?" he grumbles out. He stretches out his arm along the back of the tiny couch, and I take the opportunity to move into the space under his arm. I rest my head on his chest, and he drops his arm over my shoulder, planting a kiss on the top of my head.

"I'm sorry," I say softly, blowing out a big breath. "I got really in my head about the song, and then kind of started spiraling about us."

"I don't understand what's wrong with the song?"

"Dan, you didn't look up the plot of the show at all, did you?"

"Uh, no. Just the song lyrics," he says carefully.

I chuckle again. "Yeah, the two characters singing that song end up divorced in the end. The show is literally about how their relationship falls apart."

He groans and runs a hand down his face. "Fuck. I just thought it was a nice song." He laughs and studies me for a moment before getting serious again. "You said you were spiraling..."

I sigh and let my eyes close, gathering my nerve to respond to his unspoken question. "Things have been going well between us, but I was worried after this whole dating thing, we still might not make it work. Or we'll try again, and everything will go back to how it was before. I'm afraid to get my hopes up."

Tears sting my eyes, and Dan reaches for me, wrapping me in his arms and holding me tight.

"I'm so sorry, baby. This is all my fault." Dan surprises me with teary eyes of his own.

"It's not all your fault. It's both of our faults. I let it get so bad before I said anything. I kept secrets. It's on both of us. I'm just scared."

"Me too," he whispers into my hair.

We sit, holding each other for a long, quiet moment. The silence between us is comfortable, as we're both lost in our thoughts, thinking about our relationship. After a little while, Dan kisses my head, stands, and heads toward the door like he has after most of our dates. But tonight I can't stand the thought of him leaving again. I stand and follow him.

"Dan, wait." He turns to look at me with a questioning look on his face. "Please stay. I don't want you to leave tonight."

The atmosphere between us instantly heats as I wait for his answer.

Chapter Eighteen

Dan

I SWALLOW HARD AS I stare at Jessie. She's asking me to stay, but it's more than that. We've been avoiding sex up to this point, but the sparks flying between us right now make me think the time for going slow is over. The tension rises between us, both of us frozen, waiting to see what the other person will do.

I'm not sure who moves first, but we crash together in the middle, lips connected as I lift her off the ground. She wraps her legs around me, her small baby bump cradled between our bodies. I carry her over to the king-size bed in the corner of the apartment.

"Jessie Baby, are you sure?" I murmur. She responds by tugging on the hem of my shirt until I stand and yank it over my head.

"I need you," she says in a breathy voice, grabbing at my belt.

I push her back down onto the bed. If she gets her hands on my cock now, this won't last very long. I have to make sure she's taken care of first. I reach down to undo her jeans, but lean back when I don't find a button. I run my hand up her belly, trying to find the top of her pants.

"Where the fuck is it?" I grumble, and she chuckles.

"They're maternity jeans," she explains as she sits up and pulls her flowy red top over her head. My eyes rake over her body, taking in all the changes from the last time I saw her naked. She finds the top of the stretchy band holding up her jeans, sitting just below her round tits that have definitely gotten a lot bigger. She peels them down to reveal the most perfect, slightly rounded belly. I stare at her in stunned silence, which she immediately takes the wrong way and gets shy on me.

"I know I look different now." She's down to her bra and underwear and moves to cover herself.

I push her back down to the surface of the bed and move so my upper body is hovering over her, lying on my side. I lower my forehead to hers so the only thing she can see is my face. I need her to see the sincerity in my eyes as I tell her how hot her new body is. How badly I want her.

"Jessie. You have never been sexier than you are right now. I don't even have the words to tell you how gorgeous you are." I grind the erection, currently trying to bust through the fabric of my jeans against her hip. "Do you feel this? It's all for you. I'm doing my best not to come in my jeans at just the sight of you."

She lets out a soft moan as my hand travels down over the bump that seems to get a little bit bigger every day. I keep moving my hand down, brushing my fingers against the outside of the damp fabric between her legs.

"Are you already wet for me, baby?"

"Oh God, yes," she whimpers as I move the fabric aside and find her warm, wet center.

I circle her clit with my fingertip, bringing another low moan out of her, as she writhes against it, seeking more friction. I move lower and press one finger at her entrance, sliding into her tight heat. She squirms under my hand as I slowly thrust a second finger inside, earning me a loud gasp at the welcome intrusion.

With my free hand, I reach behind her to unclasp her bra, freeing her large, round breasts. I've known these boobs for thirteen years, and if I had any artistic abilities, I could have drawn a picture of them from memory. They're even more delicious now that they've grown in size, the nipples turning a deeper shade of pink. I lower my face, taking one nipple in a hard suck, making Jessie gasp and moan.

"Oh, fuck, they're so sensitive," she hisses as I gently bite the nipple in my mouth. I kiss my way across her chest to give the other side the same attention while picking up the pace with my hand, curling my fingers to find the spot I know makes her go crazy. I'm rewarded with her back arching off the surface of the bed, as she moans my name over and over.

With a press of my thumb to her clit, she detonates, her inner walls spasming and squeezing my fingers so hard I may have bruises tomorrow. I give her just a second to come down from her orgasm as I finally shed my pants and boxer briefs. I already know I won't last long once I'm buried inside of her. It's been too long, and there are too many emotions swirling around in my head, making every second of this feel ten times more intense than before. Fuck. It feels like the first time with her all over again.

"Dan, I need more. I need you," she breathes out, reaching for my hard cock.

"You have me," I murmur. I grab a pillow from the top of the bed and shove it under her hips to give me a better angle as I kneel between her legs. I stay upright to avoid putting too much weight on her belly. Grabbing her hips, I wrap my hands around to grip her round ass as I notch the head of my dick at her entrance.

"Oh, baby, I'm not going to last very long," I mumble as her wet heat envelopes me. I thrust slowly, letting her stretch and adjust to my size. Between the months apart and the pregnancy, she's so tight it's making me lose my mind.

I pick up the pace, thrusting more quickly as I feel her pussy squeezing and pulsing. She's close again, and her breathy moans get louder as I slam myself home, over and over. Taking us both higher and higher towards oblivion.

"Harder, please. I'm so close," she whines.

I pound into her and move my hand down to swirl around the sensitive bundle of nerves, and she falls over the edge into another orgasm. Her whole body is clenched tight, her muscles spasming around me, and it triggers my own release. My body goes still as I pour into her over and over until I'm completely spent.

I gently pull out of her and collapse onto the bed next to her. She's breathing hard as I lower my head to kiss her gently on the shoulder. She turns her head and smiles at me. She is running her hands along her baby bump. I can't resist placing my hand next to hers.

"All good?" I ask, suddenly concerned I hurt her, hurt them, with how hard we went at the end.

"Yeah, just a little tight. Orgasms cause little contractions."

"Oh, really? You say that like you have experience," I tease.

"Listen, man, pregnancy hormones are strong. I've been burning through batteries like crazy," she huffs.

We both laugh and enjoy the companionable silence. It's crazy how the chemistry between us feels both familiar and brand new. It gives me hope that this whole struggle will have us coming out the other side stronger. I already feel so much closer to her than I did before. I hope she feels the same.

I get up and grab a warm washcloth from the small bathroom, bringing it back to gently help Jessie clean up. After a quick trip to the bathroom, she crawls up to the top of the bed and gets under the covers as I throw the washcloth back in the bathroom and kill the lights. I slide into the bed behind her, wrapping my arm around her waist to rest my hand over the swell.

I kiss the top of her shoulder and think about how lucky I am that she's given me this chance to make things right. We're not one hundred percent there, but fuck if I'm going to let her walk away. Jessie is and always will be my forever.

I just have to prove it to her.

"Alright, are we ready to see your little one?" the ultrasound tech asks as she squirts the jelly on Jessie's belly.

"Yes, please!" Jessie responds excitedly, her eyes trained on the large screen mounted on the wall.

I'm holding her hand as we wait to see our baby in black and white. The image on the screen shifts until we can see a very clear profile shot of the baby's head.

Jessie gasps. "Oh my god! They actually look like a baby now!"

The tech chuckles as she plays the heartbeat over the speakers. "Heartbeat is strong at 155 bpm. I'm just gonna take some measurements as we go." She clicks some buttons on the computer, measuring the baby's head, limbs, and zooming in on organs that look like blobs to me.

I'm mesmerized by the baby's movements as it squirms around on the screen. We did this, and I'm ashamed all over again at how I could have missed everything. Jessie squeezes my hand and smiles up at me. I remind myself to stay in the present, where these two are mine and I'm not missing a single minute of it.

"Do we want to know the sex?" the tech asks. I look at Jessie to confirm we both still want to know.

"Yes, please."

"Yes, we want to know."

We respond in unison, laughing. The tech chuckles and uses the cursor to show where the baby's legs are on the screen.

"Little one's being nice and cooperative; it's a girl!"

Jessie gasps, and tears fill her eyes. "Are you sure?"

"Well, I can't promise a hundred percent, but I'm pretty sure. I'm rarely wrong on these, and I've been doing this a long time. But we can get Dr. Sharon's opinion too."

Jessie grins up at me. "A girl," she murmurs, and I lower my forehead to hers.

"A baby girl! I'm so excited. I was hoping for a girl," I whisper back.

She pulls her head back, surprised. "You said you'd be happy either way!"

"I would have, but I was secretly hoping it would be a girl. A little princess who hopefully looks just like you." I push a stray hair out of Jessie's face and tuck it behind her ears before placing a chaste kiss on her lips. She smiles at me through teary eyes.

"You're going to spoil her rotten, aren't you?" Jessie huffs a laugh.

"Of course, she's Daddy's little girl."

"We'll just have to make sure the next one's a boy so I can have a Mama's boy," Jessie says sarcastically. I see the moment she realizes what she said.

Hope bursts in my chest. She's envisioning future children, a future life with me. I don't push my luck by calling it out. I can already see her chewing her bottom lip as she looks deep in thought. She clearly surprised herself with the thought, and I'm not gonna rush her. I squeeze her hand and smile.

We pass the next few minutes watching our little girl wiggle around the screen in comfortable silence, both of us focusing on our own thoughts of what this future will look like. From where I'm sitting, it's looking like a wonderful life.

Jessie's taking pictures of the ultrasound printouts as we drive away from the doctor's office and texting them to my mom and our friends.

"What do you think about getting food and taking it back to the house?" I ask tentatively. She hasn't been back to the house since she left, but we have to cross this hurdle sometime.

She hesitates for just a second before nodding and saying, "Yeah, that works. What do you want to get?"

"I'm good with anything. What does Baby Girl want?" I shoot her a smile, still excited to know what we're having, and she grins back, rubbing her belly.

"Hmm, she's feeling sushi, but it's against the stupid pregnancy rules," Jessie whines.

"You can have sushi as long as it's not the raw stuff and you trust the place." She gapes at me in surprise. "I was doing some reading on pregnancy and found a myth-buster list from an OBGYN. It's all about avoiding foodborne illness, not necessarily sushi being bad for the baby. What?"

"I'm just surprised. I would never have expected you to do pregnancy research," she says in an astonished voice.

"It's the baby tracking app all over again," I grumble, annoyed at her surprise, even though I know she's probably right.

"I'm sorry. I just... You have to admit this all feels out of character for you. You've   never shown much interest in anything other than baseball in the past."

I nod, trying to shake off the shame her words bring. She's not wrong, and I'm realizing   how self-obsessed I've been over the last ten years. The more we talk about the past, the more I understand how she could walk away.

"It's okay, baby. You're probably right. I'm not sure I would've been as invested if your leaving hadn't opened my eyes to everything I could miss out on, and I'm sorry."

"I'm not complaining. It's nice to feel like you're really in this with me." She gives me a soft smile, and I smile back, hanging onto the hope she'll see, I *am completely* in this with her.

"Now, let's get you and our baby girl some sushi. I saw they just opened a Fusion over by the Kroger. This way, you can build-your-own sushi without any raw fish."

She nods and murmurs agreement, but she's still staring at me like she's trying to figure me out. I hate that I went so long without putting in the effort she deserves.

We get our sushi to go and head back toward the house. I've been working hard on my house projects. I hope she's happy with the changes I've made, and I can't wait to show her. Hopefully, my interest in DIY projects isn't coming too late. I've actually enjoyed everything I've done so far. I can't wait for her to put her creative touches on everything.

We pull up to the house, and she takes a deep breath before getting out of the car. I can tell she's nervous to be here, but hopefully I can help calm some of those nerves by showing her this isn't the same lonely house I left her in all those months ago.

Chapter Nineteen

Jessie

IT'S A STRANGE FEELING walking into this house with Dan. The last time we were here, I was packing a bag and leaving him for the second time, so sure I'd never live here again. The house holds so many painful memories. But on the other hand, it holds some magical ones. When we moved to Fort Starling, we knew it would be permanent, so we bought our dream house. Our forever home. Could it still be home for us?

I shoot Dan a nervous smile as we wander into the dining room, and I instantly stop in my tracks with a gasp. On what was once a blank space is a full gallery wall of picture frames. The frames are different shapes and sizes but are all painted a soft metallic rose gold color. The wall behind the frames has been painted a perfect soft mauve. Most of the frames have pictures of us with our friends and family over the years. A few have been left empty.

It's exactly what I envisioned for this wall, but I never got around to doing it because I hate painting walls. Dan always said I should hire someone, but it always felt like he was brushing me off, not even listening to what I wanted for our home. Yeah, I could have hired someone, but I wanted us to make these changes ourselves. It was on my list of someday projects. Ones I was waiting and hoping for Dan to miraculously show an interest in.

I turn to look at Dan and find him already watching me with a wary look in his eyes. He's waiting to hear my reaction to the wall, and it's clear he's nervous.

"It's exactly what I wanted. How did you know?" I murmur as I move toward him.

"I was always listening when you talked about house projects, Jess. I was just shitty about showing it. I'm sorry I didn't make more time for the things you wanted before."

Tears fill my eyes as I wrap my arms around his waist. "Thank you," I whisper, my forehead resting on his chest.

"I left some frames empty so we can fill them with pictures of Baby Girl."

It's such a thoughtful sentiment. He's trying so hard. I want to believe that if we give this another try, things will stay this way, but I'm still so scared that everything will go right back to the way it was. I'm still not sure how to trust him.

We sit in the dining room while we eat our sushi bowls. I ordered mine with a yummy teriyaki steak, giving me the sushi flavor and vibes without the risk of getting sick and hurting the munchkin. The whole time I eat, I can't stop looking at the beautiful wall. There's not a thing about it I would change. He matched my vision perfectly. When we're done eating, Dan stands up and reaches for my hand.

"Come here; there are a couple of other things I want to show you."

He takes my hand and pulls me to the guest bathroom off the living room. I gasp   again as I take in the changes he's made. The flooring is different, and he had the tub replaced with a shower stall, so there's more space in front of the toilet and vanity. I always complained about the bathroom being too cramped for a full tub.

"This was the flooring you wanted, right?" he asks carefully.

"Yeah. Did you do this yourself?"

He nods, leaning against the doorframe. "Bailey and Griffin helped with the flooring, and I hired someone for the shower. I didn't think it was a good idea for me to be messing with plumbing."

I laugh and shake my head in awe. He pulls my hand toward the stairs.

"There's more?" I ask, surprised he's been able to make so many changes to our house in just a couple of months.

"Just one more," he says quietly as he opens the door to the guest room closest to the master. "I haven't done much in here yet, because I figured you'd want to pick everything out, especially now that we know the sex of the baby."

I stop in the doorway to see find all of the furniture that was in here before has been moved out. The walls are prepped for painting, and there's a small pile of baby things in the closet.

Until this moment, I haven't wanted to even think about a nursery for the baby, not knowing if we'd be living at the Songbird apartment or possibly finding something else. Everything feels too up in the air to picture where our baby will come home.

"You're setting up a nursery?" I ask softly.

"I was hoping we'd be setting it up together," Dan says with a sad shrug. "But even if we, uh, if things don't... she'll need somewhere to stay when she's with me."

His words hit hard. *Fuck* this is so complicated. I don't want to pass our baby back and forth, but I also don't want to stay in an unhappy marriage just for her sake. What kind of example would it set for her?

But what if the marriage isn't unhappy anymore? Can I trust this new version of Dan is going to be the one that sticks? Or will I be going through all of this again down the road?

I wish I knew.

We sat in the nursery for a while, coming up with ideas of how to decorate it now that we know we're having a girl. I pulled open my Pinterest, and we scrolled for a while, pinning things we loved and imagining our little girl in this space. After the third time I let out an enormous yawn, Dan gets up off the floor and helps me to stand.

"Do you want me to take you back to the Songbird, or do you want to stay here tonight?" He brushes my loose hair behind my ear and smiles down at me.

"I want to stay here." I push up onto my toes to kiss him. He bends to deepen the kiss, and we slowly back our way out of the room and next door to the bedroom we shared for the four years we've owned this house. It's both strange and comfortable to be back in this room with him.

Dan backs me up until my legs hit the bed. He reaches for the hem of my dress and pulls it up over my head, leaving me in a matching lace bra and panty set. I had a feeling we'd be finding the bedroom at some point today, so I dressed for it. Dan lets out a low chuckle as he takes in the pink lace.

"Baby, you're like a not-safe-for-work gender reveal right now."

It takes me a hot second to figure out what he means, but when I do, I bark out a laugh. He's right; my petal pink lingerie has major "it's a girl" vibes. Little does he know, I almost went with a cobalt blue set this morning. The thought only makes me laugh harder.

"I guess I was manifesting a girl," I say in between giggles.

"It worked," Dan murmurs into the skin along my neck as he reaches behind my back to undo my bra. All thoughts of the baby are suddenly far away as he kisses his way down my neck and across my collarbone. He cups my breasts in his large hands, gently running his thumbs over my aching nipples.

"Are these still sensitive?" he asks, just before lowering his mouth to one nipple. He rolls and pinches the other before switching, giving them equal attention.

"Yes," I moan out as he gently presses my shoulder so I'm lying back on the bed, and I scoot my way up to the top of the bed, making room for him between my legs. Once I'm situated, he resumes kissing his way down my body and making his way down across my round belly.

He lowers himself to his stomach between my legs and hooks his fingers in the sides of my lace panties, pulling them down painfully slowly. I gasp when his warm breath grazes my clit, and he pulls my legs over his shoulders. My gasps turn to moans as he buries his head between my legs.

He flicks my clit with fast strokes of his tongue as he slides two fingers deep into my core. The way he's devouring my pussy has me writhing and moaning so loud, if we had neighbors close by, they'd be complaining.

"Oh, fuck, Dan, I'm so close," I scream out. His grip on my ass tightens, and he lets out a low growl, never slowing his pace. The vibration tips me over the edge, and my world shatters around me. Every muscle in my body tenses as I ride out wave after wave of the most powerful orgasm I've ever had.

Dan kisses his way back up my body as I come down, still breathing hard. He lies down next to me and rests his hand on the swell of my bump, rising and falling as I catch my breath. He kisses my shoulder and leans his forehead against my temple. I roll my head to look at him, and the pure adoration in his eyes makes my breath hitch.

We stare into each other's eyes in silence for a long moment that feels like it stretches on forever. Finally, we both move together as he lies flat and I swing my leg over to straddle him. Wordlessly, we hold eye contact as I reach down to line him up at my entrance. We groan together as I sink down, taking him to the hilt in one smooth movement.

"Fuck, Jessie Baby, you feel so good." He grips my hips hard as he thrusts up into me, stealing my breath each time as I ride him, chasing another release.

"So do you," I pant into his mouth as he sits up to wrap his arms around me. His fingers thread into my hair, holding my face to his. He presses his forehead to mine, eyes clenched shut.

"I missed you so much," he whimpers, voice filled with pain.

Tears slip down my face as I kiss him hard, words failing me.

We rock together, climbing higher until he threads his hand between us to stroke two fingers across the sensitive bundle of nerves, detonating my release. My orgasm triggers his, and we both stay locked together, riding out the intensity of the waves.

After we've both come down, we move quietly to the bathroom, showering together, tenderly washing each other. The peaceful quiet envelopes us as we get ready for bed and climb under the covers together.

As he wraps his arms around me, one large hand resting across my bump, I replay the night. Something feels different between us. Like a joint that was out of alignment has finally slipped back into place. The relief is intense, but the pain hasn't quite faded away. In fact, it may still hurt for quite a while, but it's a sign of healing.

I finally drift off, praying fervently that the healing can last and we won't fall apart all over again when things get difficult. I want to trust everything has changed, that we've changed.

I want to believe it so badly.

Chapter Twenty

Dan

SINCE WE HAVE COUNSELING the next morning, we decide to ride together. We stop at Songbird so Jessie can change clothes. Hopefully, soon she'll be moving back home. Last night felt like it unlocked some of the tension between us. It feels like we're moving in the right direction, but she's been quiet this morning, which of course makes me nervous as fuck.

Theresa ushers us into her office, and we take our usual seats, waiting for Theresa to start. I watch Jessie out of the corner of my eye. She's playing with the hem of the pink sundress she put on. She looks worried, and my stomach clenches again with nerves. Did I misread everything last night?

"So, how's everything going? It's been a couple of weeks since we've talked, with me being on vacation last week. How's the dating going?"

Jessie glances up at me and gives me a timid smile before she turns to Theresa. "It's been good. It feels like we're connecting better, and we've had some big conversations."

"Excellent. Dan, how are you feeling about the dating?"

I nod and agree with Jessie. "It's been good, amazing actually. It feels like old times."

Jessie flinches, and I know I've said the wrong thing, but I don't exactly know what. Theresa, being the incredibly perceptive lady she is, homes in on Jessie's reaction.

"Jessie, you seemed to react strongly to what Dan said. Do you want to share?"

Jessie blows out a big breath, her forehead furrowing as she chooses her words. "Dan's right; it has felt like old times. When we first started dating, we were so connected, so in sync. It was amazing, and I was so incredibly happy." She pauses, and the "but" hanging in the air makes my whole body tense. "But... over the years, it went away. We got caught up in our own shit. We didn't communicate, we broke promises, and I guess I'm so afraid that if we decide to give this another try, we'll just end up back in this exact same place. Only then, we'll have another tiny person who will be dragged into everything. One who could be hurt and emotionally damaged in the process."

"Dan, any response?" Theresa asks with her eyebrows raised.

I clear my throat. I don't know how to convince her, I'm not gonna risk losing her again, but I have to try. "I know we—I—didn't do the best job of making our marriage a priority before. I fucked up and didn't value us the way I should have. I will regret it for the rest of my life. But I will *never* make the same mistake again. I'm sure I'll make new mistakes, but I won't risk losing you, Jess. You and the baby are my number one priority, and nothing will ever come before you again."

Jessie swipes at the tears running down her face. "I want to believe you. I want to believe you so badly it hurts. I'm trying."

Theresa pushes the box of tissues toward her, and Jessie grabs one and wipes at her face.

"Jessie, what makes it hard for you to believe Dan?"

She sniffles. "I believe he means what he says. I'm just afraid that when things get hard, he'll backtrack. It'll be like every other broken promise he's made over the years. I don't know how to trust him anymore."

Her words hit hard. I know I deserve it, but *fuck;* I thought we were making some real progress.

"It's the tricky thing about broken trust. It has to be rebuilt. It's not something you can repair overnight. Trust has to be earned," Theresa says kindly but firmly.

I nod and look over at Jessie. "I get why you don't trust what I say. I know I let you down. I'm just asking for a chance to earn your trust again."

"I know." She reaches out and squeezes my hand. She gives me a sad smile. "But it's not just about me. I need to be sure. I need more time."

Theresa interjects, "You don't have to make any decisions until you're ready. We're playing the long game here instead of looking for quick fixes. It seems like you're at least open to the idea of reconciliation? I know you were unsure in the beginning, Jessie."

Jessie nods. "I'm open to it. Honestly, it's what I want deep down. I just feel so blocked up by the trust issue. I can't quite let go of the fear that everything will go back to the way things were once we're comfortable and back in the flow of everyday life, and I don't think I could stand it."

We spend the rest of the hour discussing communication and keeping ourselves open to each other. I'm taking it all in, but my mind also keeps wandering, trying to come up with a way to show her how much I've changed through all of this. It's like finding the journal, seeing the way she experienced each of those years, opened my eyes.

It shifted something in my brain, and there's no going back. I almost lost the most important person in my life because I wasn't paying attention. Too caught up in my own wants and needs to realize the love of my life was begging for me to see her. Not to sound too cliché, but I will make her see I would rather die than let her feel neglected again, if it's the last thing I do.

It may be time to call in some reinforcements.

I walk into the Songbird Café a week later, knowing Jessie is out working on a business luncheon event she had on her calendar. I'm not here to see Jessie. I'm here to beg Leena and Annie for their help. Knowing these ladies and their fierce protectiveness, it's going to be a hard sell.

They're both already there. Leena is behind the bar pouring a drink for Annie, who is perched on a stool. Cass is here too, clearly doing some sort of inventory on a clipboard, but with the way her body is aimed toward the others, I have a feeling she'll be giving her opinion as well.

I clear my throat, feeling like I'm walking into a lion's den. "Hello, ladies. Thanks for meeting me."

Annie gives me a tentative smile. She's got her light brown hair pulled into a ponytail and is wearing a Reynolds PT polo, so she must have come straight from the practice she now owns with Eric. She's always been the friendlier one of this crew, and I slide onto the barstool next to her.

Leena has always been snarky and a little grumpy, even before all the shit she went through a few years ago. Even now, being happily engaged to

Bailey doesn't seem to have changed her disposition much unless Bailey's around. She lights up when he's in the room, and I'm glad to see them both so happy.

I don't know Cass as well since she and Jessie weren't close before, but she's pretty much Leena's personality twin. They look like total opposites, with Leena's wild red curls and short, curvy stature contrasting with Cass's tall, willowy frame and bluntly cut bob of black hair. Right now, though, they're both looking at me with the same wary expression.

I clear my throat. "I think you're all pretty aware of everything happening between me and Jessie." I glance at the three of them to see them nodding. Leena narrows her eyes and waits for me to continue. "I, uh, I could use your advice."

All three sets of eyebrows shoot up. In all the years Jessie and I have been together, I've never asked for their opinions on anything. Not her engagement ring, not my proposal plan, not any birthday or Christmas gift idea. I probably should have come to them a million times over the years. Maybe we wouldn't be in this mess now if I had been willing to put in the energy before.

"It's about fucking time," Leena grumbles accusingly. "I've been waiting for you to consult us about Jessie for the last thirteen years."

I blow out a big puff of air, clutching my patience with both hands. "I know. I should have."

"Alright," Annie interjects in a friendly tone while giving Leena a wide-eyed look. "Let's focus on how we can help now."

I nod and lay it out for them. "Things have been better between me and Jess, but she still doesn't trust me. Which is totally understandable, I know I need to earn her trust back... but I thought you guys might have some ideas on better ways to show her I won't ever take her for granted again."

The hostility from Leena and Cass seems to go down a few notches, and Annie smiles at me. "Well, it sounds like you're on the right path so far. She's been pretty impressed by the house projects and how invested you've been in the baby."

Leena comes around the bar and sits on the other side of me. "She mentioned you've put more effort into knowing what she's doing at work, too. Remembering her schedule and asking how work was, the kind of things you were shitty at before," she says in a begrudging tone.

I huff a laugh at her inability to sugarcoat things. "So you think I just keep doing what I'm doing? It doesn't feel like enough." I run my hands through my hair, feeling frustrated that I can't just fix everything. There's a long beat of silence, each of us focused on our own thoughts.

"You gotta give her a way to see what you're thinking," Cass finally murmurs, breaking the silence. All three of our heads snap up to look at her. She shrugs. "She likes the gestures, but what she's really afraid of is that you're all talk like you were before. She's afraid you're blowing smoke up her ass just to win her over, and you'll go back on it all when you get comfortable again. You have to find a way to reassure her you won't make the same mistakes again."

"Shit, you're right. I thought you and Jessie weren't even friends!" Leena exclaims.

Cass rolls her eyes. "We were never *not* friends, we just weren't that close before," she says with a shrug. "She lives here. I'm always here. We've gotten to know each other better over the last few months."

"So you're saying I need to show her I'm not just making promises. Show her I mean it. How do I do that? I can't get her to read my mind... wait." They all look at me expectantly. "I know how I can show her what I'm really thinking. Any other suggestions? Big grand gesture style?"

"You could upgrade her engagement ring?"

I snap my head to look at Annie. She came up with the ring idea awfully quickly. I raise my eyebrows for her to elaborate.

She shrugs, and instead, it's Leena who fills me in. "It's just not what she always wanted, but she loves you, so she never wanted to hurt your feelings by telling you she didn't want a round solitaire in yellow gold. She likes a princess cut or something more square in white gold. Should have asked us before you bought it!"

I run my hand down my face. *Fuck.* Every time I think I've got a grip on all the mistakes I've made, I find another one. "Well, shit. I'll fix it. Do any of you know where she's been keeping it? She, uh, hasn't worn it in a while."

Annie shoots me a sympathetic glance as Leena hops down from her stool and disappears into the kitchen. A few minutes later, she comes back and sets Jessie's modest solitaire and the plain band soldered to it in front of me on the bar. Shit, just looking at the set makes it obvious she's needed an upgrade for a long time, and I swallow down the guilt that I didn't notice.

"Thanks, Leens."

"Sure, do you need help taking it to the jeweler? Her Pinterest would honestly be the best place to start."

"Right... Pinterest. We were on Jessie's the other day looking at nursery stuff. How do I find hers?" Minutes later, after some eye rolling, I'm the owner of my own Pinterest account. Now I'm scrolling through Jessie's boards, feeling like I've got a window into her brain. They're giving me a million ideas of ways I can prove to her I'm paying attention. Prove how I only want to give her the best.

I thank the girls and leave Songbird armed with a plan. It'll take me a few weeks to execute, but hopefully, when I'm done, Jessie will know I will never take her for granted again.

Chapter Twenty-One
Jessie

DAN'S BEEN QUIET FOR the last few weeks, ever since I balked at the topic of getting back together at counseling. We've still been going on dates and seeing each other on counseling days, and the sex has been out of this world amazing. Thank you, pregnancy hormones. But we haven't circled back to the conversation. I keep waiting for him to bring it up, to ask again, but he doesn't. I don't know if it's because he's giving me space to trust him again or if it's because he's giving up hope.

I'm regretting turning down getting back together when I had the chance. Maybe then we'd at least be working on all of this together in our home. I haven't been back to the house since the day we discussed it all at counseling, almost three weeks ago. I miss the feeling of coming home that had less to do with the house than with the other person in it.

I'm nervous as I'm getting ready for him to pick me up for our date tonight. With our anniversary coming up this week, I have a gut feeling something's going to happen tonight, and I can't decide if it's good or bad. What if he doesn't want to try anymore? What if he's tired of me dragging my feet on trusting him?

I take another look in the full-length mirror in the corner, smoothing my light peach dress over my belly. It has a pretty geometric pattern and a deep V neckline showing off my huge pregnancy boobs. Plus, the bump is bumpin' tonight, and the flowy dress shows it off even more. As soon as I hit twenty-five weeks, it's like the baby popped way out, making it obvious I'm pregnant now.

I'm a little tempted to put my rings back on, but I bite my cheek and do my best to ignore my parents' voices in my head harping on appearances. I'll put my rings back on when and if Dan and I figure out our shit. I move to my jewelry box to look at them, but they're not there. I could have sworn I put them in there when I moved all my stuff over, but maybe I left them at the house. I shake off my confusion as a knock sounds at the door. I'll worry about my rings later.

I open the door to find Dan holding a gorgeous bouquet filled with all of my favorite wildflowers. He's wearing dark jeans and a tight navy blue t-shirt, making the green in his eyes   more vibrant. He smiles down at me, but he's giving off a nervous energy as he hands me the flowers and kisses me on the cheek.

"Thank you; these are beautiful."

"So are you. How are my girls doing?" he asks as he lowers his hands to my bump.

"We're mostly good," I reply as I fill a vase with water and arrange the flowers on the small kitchen table.

"Mostly?"

"It's getting a little tricky to sleep. She's pressing on my bladder, so I get up to pee a bunch of times in the night, and getting up isn't as easy as it used to be."

"Ah, got it. Anything I can do to help?"

I smile up at him. Just him asking how he can help is a change from how he would have reacted before. I gave up complaining about anything a long time ago. He would usually brush me off or one-up my complaints with his own until I was too annoyed to continue the conversation.

"I don't think so. Pretty sure it's only gonna get worse as we hit the third trimester in a few weeks."

"You'll let me know if you think of something?"

I nod and give him another big smile. I don't know why I've been dragging my feet. It's so clear this is not the man he became during our marriage. He's more present and aware than he's ever been. Maybe it's time we moved forward for real.

I don't know how to bring the subject up again, though, so I follow him out the door and down the stairs. He waits at the bottom for me, watching me as I navigate the stairs more slowly. Not being able to see my feet makes me nervous.

He smiles and grabs my hand as we maneuver through the bar and out into the soft light of the summer evening, heading toward his car. When he pulls away from downtown, I ask what the plan for dinner is.

"I actually prepped dinner at the house. Just have to do some finishing touches and grill the chicken."

This man is turning surprising me into his new life's calling. I can count on one hand the times Dan has made me a meal. Ordering takeout? Sure. But actually prepping and cooking a meal? No way.

"What did you make?" I ask, curiosity dripping from my voice.

"You'll just have to wait and see, Jessie Baby." He grins at me, shoots me a wink, and reaches over to squeeze my knee, and I'm hit with a flood of happiness, surprising in its intensity.

If you had told me six months ago we'd be here like this today, I would have said you were nuts. I thought we'd be divorced by now. I figured I'd be trying to rearrange the pieces of my heart that had been slowly broken over the last few years. Trying to move on. I never dreamed we'd have a second chance instead.

It's what this is. Our second chance, and I shouldn't let more time go by without telling him. I want to come home for good, not just for dinner. Tonight's the night. After we eat whatever mystery meal he's come up with, we'll have the talk about putting us back together.

After a quick stop at the bathroom because this baby loves to use my bladder as her own personal trampoline, I find Dan in the kitchen pulling a bowl of chicken thighs covered in a dark marinade out of the fridge.

"I already put the salads out on the table, and I'm gonna get the chicken going on the grill. Can you grab the lemonade?" He nods a head toward the fridge and moves toward the back door and slips through it. My eyes follow him, but I'm frozen in confusion.

Are we eating outside? Last I checked, we had a shitty glass-top table and some rickety chairs out there. It works in a pinch for holding my stuff when I'm out there tanning or on the rare occasion I want to sit outside to read, but it certainly isn't a space for eating.

I shake my head and grab the pitcher of lemonade from the shelf in the fridge.

Stepping through the door, the shocking sight of our backyard almost makes me lose my grip on the pitcher. Luckily, Dan is beside me to take it out of my hands like he knew I'd be stunned. I look up at him to find him beaming a smile down at me.

Our backyard has been completely transformed. If I hadn't come through our house, I wouldn't believe it was the same backyard. Instead of a simple set of stairs leading out onto a twelve-foot square of concrete like it used to, the door opens to a gorgeous new deck extending the length of the house and out into the yard.

I gaze at the expanse of the yard in awe. Flower beds, overflowing with greenery and color, have been installed in front of the tall hedges lining the sides of the yard to mark the property lines. The hedges used to be a boring alternative to a fence, but now they've become the walls to my own secret garden.

My bench swing that lives in the middle of the yard, the only decorative piece I insisted on when we moved here, has been transformed with a beautiful trellis over the top. Small ivy plants climb the sides, and I can already picture the way the ivy will look in a few years.

String lights have been installed over the top of the deck, with another strand decorating the swing's trellis. Dan reaches into the house and flips the switch for what used to be a simple porch light, and the whole yard lights up. The tears that have been lingering in my eyes since I stepped outside slide down my face at the sight.

"You... How did you..." I stammer, trying to find the question I want answered first. "It's like you read my mind on what I wanted back here. How did you know?"

He shrugs before answering sheepishly, "Your Pinterest had a lot of options to choose from, so I just picked some of the common threads. You like it?"

"Like it," I scoff, shaking my head. "Dan, I love it. It's the most beautiful backyard I've ever seen. I couldn't have designed it better myself. Did you do all of this?"

"I helped with a lot of it. I hired out the deck; I didn't want to fuck it up. But I did the flower beds, and Bailey helped me install the trellis over the swing."

"It's amazing. I can see her playing back here."

"I left a space for a swing set over there," he says, pointing to an empty section of the yard. "I figured we have a while until she'll need it, and I didn't want it getting weathered in the meantime."

"I can't believe you did this," I murmur, shaking my head in awe. There are so many new details to look at in this yard, I can hardly focus on one before something new catches my eye.

"Let's eat, and we can talk more," Dan says softly. He tips his head toward a new outdoor dining table placed in the center of the deck. As I'm sitting down, I'm noticing the fireplace built into the front of the deck and the comfortable-looking outdoor sectional positioned in front of it. Those are gonna get a ton of use as my new favorite reading spot as we move toward fall.

We eat quietly, both of us focused on our own thoughts. We share small smiles, but conversation is minimal. If I hadn't already decided I wanted to come home, this backyard would have clinched it. The Dan of before, even in our best days, would never have gone to this much effort. Not only to remodel the backyard, but to figure out what I would want.

I'm stunned by this new version of him, and I'm just going to trust that this is going to last. He'll keep showing up for us. I can't keep putting him off because of my fear of the past repeating itself. I clear my throat and set my napkin down.

"This is really wonderful, Dan."

"I'm sorry it took so long."

"Eh, the yard was lower on my list of home projects," I say with a chuckle.

"Not what I meant," he says seriously. "I'm sorry it took me so long to see there was more you needed from me."

I swallow hard, tears filling my eyes. It's everything I've needed him to say. I sniffle and nod my head, words failing me. He stands and pulls me up to follow him. We sit side by side on the couch. He reaches behind him and holds a small package in his hand.

"I found this, and it honestly was hard to read about all the ways I'd been failing you for years."

I gasp when I realize what he's holding. The small white journal his mom gave us as a wedding present is held in his grasp. The little book I spilled my guts into each year. The one I thought he'd never look at again after I had to practically beg him to write in it when we were first married.

The one he refused to write in the next year, and I started using as a place to dump all of my frustration about our marriage.

I never dreamed he'd read it. It should have been in one of the boxes I packed up from my office, and I can't believe I left it behind. I can feel the blood draining from my face. I can't even remember all the things I wrote in there.

"Dan. I never meant for you to read all of those. It was just for me to vent," I whisper through the lump in my throat.

"I know, and I'm sorry I read it without your permission. I figured some of it was you letting off some steam. But I think you wrote some things here instead of telling me, so you could protect my feelings. You knew I would take any disappointments you had personally."

I swallow hard. He may have been overlooking me these last few years, but he still knows me better than anyone. It's exactly why my complaints went in a journal he would never see. I'm about to launch into another explanation when he speaks up again.

"I thought maybe I could give you my perspective on those years."

My head snaps up to look at him. He gives me a soft smile, hands me the journal, and stands up. He leans down to plant a kiss on my forehead.

"I'll get dinner cleaned up while you read."

I blow out a big breath in an attempt to mentally prepare myself to dive into the last ten years. I'm not sure I'm ready to relive all of my own experiences, and I know Dan's thoughts on them are sure to wreck me. But this feels necessary. This feels like exactly what we need to put all of our broken pieces back together, so I take a deep breath and open the journal.

The first entries from our wedding day are unchanged. I smile to remember how happy we were then. I turn the page to find Dan's writing under mine on the first-year entry.

From the Anniversary Journal of: Dan & Jessie Chase (Dan's Version)

Year One

His:

Jessie still! I don't think Dan's gonna write in this thing. I asked him to, but he said he didn't have time. Oh well! This journal can just be for me to look back on our memories! Maybe I'll use it to vent about the silly things I get frustrated with Dan about, and then it'll be funny to read my whining when we're old and gray!

JESSIE BABY,

FIRST, I'M SORRY I BLEW OFF WRITING IN THIS JOURNAL. I SHOULD HAVE MADE IT A PRIORITY. IT WAS CLEARLY IMPORTANT TO YOU, AND I DIDN'T MAKE THE TIME. THE FIRST YEAR IN THE MAJORS WAS INTENSE.

YOU KNEW I WAS STRESSED, BUT THE PRESSURE OF MOVING UP AND MAKING SURE I WAS GOOD ENOUGH TO STAY WAS OVERWHELMING.

I REMEMBER TAKING ON EXTRA PRACTICES TO KEEP MY SKILLS GROWING WHEN I SHOULD HAVE BEEN HOME. THE OLDER GUYS USED TO TELL ME I SHOULD HEAD HOME TO MY WIFE, BUT I WAS SO FOCUSED ON PROVIDING FOR YOU FINANCIALLY. I LET IT CONSUME ME AND TOLD MYSELF YOU'D RATHER HAVE ME OUT EARNING OUR LIVING AND IT DIDN'T MATTER IF I HELPED YOU DECORATE. I TOLD MYSELF EXTRA PRACTICES WERE MORE VALUABLE THAN DOWNTIME WITH YOU.

I WAS WRONG.

I WAS SO WRONG. AND THIS IS WHAT STANDS OUT MOST IN RETIREMENT. BASEBALL WAS ALWAYS GOING TO BE TEMPORARY, BUT YOU AND I WERE SUPPOSED TO BE FOREVER. I GOT MY PRIORITIES WRONG FROM THE BEGINNING, AND I'LL ALWAYS BE SORRY. I SWEAR I'VE GOT THEM FIGURED OUT NOW.

I LOVE YOU.

Year Two

His:

JESSIE BABY,

I HAVE A FEELING ALL OF MY ENTRIES HERE ARE GOING TO HAVE TO START WITH I'M SORRY. I'M SORRY YOU FELT LIKE I DIDN'T CARE ABOUT WHAT WAS GOING ON IN YOUR LIFE. I'VE ALWAYS CARED, BUT I CLEARLY HAD A SHITTY WAY OF SHOWING IT. I'M SORRY I LET THE PRESSURE OF BEING NEW ON A TEAM GET IN THE WAY OF MAKING YOU FEEL YOU WERE THE MOST IMPORTANT THING TO ME. BECAUSE YOU ALWAYS HAVE BEEN. YOU ALWAYS WILL BE. YOU AND BABY GIRL ARE MY ENTIRE WORLD.

I'M SO GLAD YOU HAD MY MOM DURING THOSE YEARS. I KNOW SHE'S JUST AS GRATEFUL FOR YOUR RELATIONSHIP AS YOU WERE. IT WAS JUST THE TWO OF US FOR SO LONG, SO SHE'S ALWAYS LOVED HAVING YOU IN HER LIFE. THE DAUGHTER SHE NEVER HAD. THANK

YOU FOR NOT TAKING THAT AWAY FROM HER WHILE
WE'VE BEEN HAVING TROUBLE.

I REMEMBER THE YEARS IN CHARLOTTE BEING WON-
DERFUL. IT FELT LIKE YOU WERE REALLY HAPPY
THERE, AND I COULD BREATHE EASIER AND FOCUS
MORE ON BASEBALL. IT RELIEVED SOME OF THE GUILT
I HAD OVER ADDING EXTRA PRACTICES AND WORK-
OUTS KNOWING YOU WERE HAPPY WITH MY MOM AND
GWEN THERE. I SHOULD HAVE MADE MORE TIME FOR
US.

AND JUST FOR THE RECORD, I'VE ALWAYS BEEN
PROUD OF THE WORK YOU'VE DONE WITH JC EVENTS.
I'M NOT SURE HOW MANY PEOPLE I TOLD ABOUT
YOUR BUSINESS, BUT IT WAS A LOT. ANYONE WHO EVER
MENTIONED NEEDING TO PLAN A PARTY, I TOLD THEM
ABOUT YOU. I SHOULD HAVE TOLD YOU I WAS BRAGGING
ABOUT YOU. YOU DESERVED TO KNOW HOW PROUD I'VE
ALWAYS BEEN OF YOU.

I LOVE YOU.

Year Three

His:

JESSIE BABY,

AS MUCH AS I'M STILL ANNOYED YOU KEPT THE TRUST FUND INFO FROM ME, I GET WHY YOU DID. YOU WERE PROBABLY RIGHT, THE PRESSURE OF IT WOULD HAVE GONE TO MY HEAD. I WAS SO FOCUSED ON PROVIDING FOR US; I LET IT BECOME THE MOST IMPORTANT THING IN THE WORLD. I HATE THAT YOU THOUGHT YOU HAD TO HIDE THINGS FROM ME TO PROTECT MY FEELINGS. I WANT YOU TO KNOW YOU NEVER HAVE TO KEEP ANYTHING FROM ME IN THE FUTURE. I WANT TO KNOW ANYTHING AND EVERYTHING YOU'RE FEELING.

I HAD NO IDEA YOU WERE THINKING ABOUT BABIES THIS EARLY ON. WHEN GWEN AND MARCUS HAD GRAYSON, ALL I COULD THINK WAS, "THANK GOD WE'RE NOT THERE YET." THE IDEA OF A BABY STILL MADE ME SO NERVOUS. ANOTHER PERSON TO PRO-

VIDE FOR ANOTHER PERSON TO WORRY ABOUT. I HAD NO IDEA GRAYSON'S ARRIVAL IN OUR FRIEND GROUP MADE YOU WANT ONE, AND I'M SORRY THE WAY I ACTED WHEN I WAS HOME MADE YOU FEEL LIKE YOU COULDN'T HAVE WHAT YOU WANTED.

I KNOW IT'S NOT HOW WE PLANNED IT, BUT YOU WERE RIGHT, IT WOULD HAVE BEEN TERRIBLE FOR ME TO MISS SO MUCH OF THE BABY PROCESS. I'VE LOVED EVERY MOMENT I'VE GOTTEN TO EXPERIENCE, EVERY DOCTOR APPOINTMENT. I WANT TO BE THERE FOR EVERY SINGLE SECOND I CAN.

I LOVE YOU.

Year Four

His:

JESSIE BABY,

I DIDN'T KNOW JUST HOW HARD CALIFORNIA WAS FOR YOU. I KNEW YOU WEREN'T AS HAPPY THERE AS YOU WERE IN CHARLOTTE, BUT I DIDN'T REALIZE HOW MISERABLE YOU WERE. EITHER WAY, I KNEW YOU BEING UNHAPPY WAS MY FAULT. I'M THE ONE WHO GOT TRADED. I'M THE ONE WHO WAS RESPONSIBLE FOR US HAVING TO MOVE ACROSS THE COUNTRY AND LEAVE ALL OUR FRIENDS AND MY MOM.

I FELT LIKE I HAD TO DOUBLE DOWN ON MY FOCUS ON BASEBALL TO MAKE SURE THE TRADE WAS WORTH IT. I'M SORRY I WAS BLIND TO THE FACT THAT I COULD HAVE MADE THINGS BETTER JUST BY BEING AROUND MORE AND BEING MORE AWARE OF WHAT YOU NEEDED. I GOT HAVING A BABY INTO MY HEAD AS A WAY TO GIVE YOU SOMETHING ELSE TO FOCUS ON, BUT

I DIDN'T REALIZE HOW HARD IT WOULD BE WITHOUT THE SUPPORT SYSTEM WE HAVE HERE.

I BROUGHT UP RETIREMENT, HOPING IT WOULD GIVE YOU SOMETHING TO LOOK FORWARD TO. I WAS TRYING TO BUY TIME AND MAKE YOU FEEL BETTER IN THE MOMENT, RATHER THAN FIXING THE ACTUAL PROBLEMS. I'M SORRY I BROUGHT IT UP WHEN I WASN'T REALLY READY TO RETIRE. I'M REALIZING JUST HOW DUMB IT WAS NOT TO LET YOU KNOW MY REAL FEELINGS ABOUT IT. IT ONLY CAUSED PROBLEMS. ONES I'LL BE SORRY FOR FOREVER.

I LOVE YOU.

Year Five

His:

JESSIE BABY,

I KNOW I SOUND A BIT LIKE A BROKEN RECORD
AT THIS POINT. I'M SORRY FOR NOT BEING MORE
PRESENT. YOU WENT OUT OF YOUR WAY TO TELL ME
WHAT YOU NEEDED, AND I BLEW YOU OFF SO MANY
TIMES. I TOLD MYSELF THAT FOCUSING ON REHABBING
MY SHOULDER WAS DOING WHAT WAS BEST FOR US. I
TOLD MYSELF I NEEDED TO GET BACK TO 100% SO I
COULD KEEP PROVIDING FOR US. BRINGING IN MONEY
WAS THE MOST IMPORTANT THING I COULD DO.

I'M SORRY FOR ACTING LIKE RETIREMENT WAS
SOMETHING I WAS READY FOR. FUCK, LOOKING BACK,
IT WASN'T EVEN YOUR IDEA, AND I CONVINCED MYSELF
YOU WANTED ME TO RETIRE. YOUR INSISTENCE ON
WAITING TO HAVE KIDS UNTIL I RETIRED MADE ME
FEEL LIKE YOU WERE SITTING AND WAITING FOR ME

TO GIVE UP MY DREAMS. I RESENTED YOUR WANTING TO WAIT. IT FELT LIKE YOU PUT A TICKING CLOCK ON MY CAREER.

I'M SORRY I DIDN'T SEE YOU WANTED MORE OUT OF THE FAMILY EXPERIENCE. I'M SORRY I DANGLED RETIREMENT LIKE SOME INCENTIVE TO BE HAPPY IN THE MEANTIME. IF I COULD GO BACK, I WOULD CHANGE SO MUCH ABOUT THESE CONVERSATIONS. I'M SORRY WE WENT SO LONG NOT BEING ON THE SAME PAGE.

I LOVE YOU.

Year Six

His:

Jessie Baby,

I WAS SO CONFUSED WHEN YOU WEREN'T HAPPIER WITH THE MOVE TO FORT STARLING. I THOUGHT JUST BEING HOME WOULD BE ENOUGH. I THOUGHT IT WOULD TAKE THE PRESSURE OFF ME. I COULD FOCUS ON MY LAST FEW YEARS OF BASEBALL, AND BEING HERE WOULD DISTRACT YOU. I'M SORRY I COULDN'T SEE THAT THE PROBLEMS WERE INSIDE OUR MARRIAGE. THEY WOULD HAVE FOLLOWED US NO MATTER WHERE WE LIVED, AND I COULDN'T SEE IT THEN.

WHEN I READ HOW I MADE YOU FEEL INVISIBLE, BABY, IT WRECKED ME. YOU'VE NEVER BEEN INVISIBLE TO ME. I'M SORRY I WASN'T ABLE TO BALANCE THE PRESSURE OF MY CAREER WITH WHAT YOU NEEDED. I REMEMBER THESE FIGHTS, AND I WAS SO CAUGHT UP IN PROVING MYSELF ON THE FIELD. I PUT OFF MAKING

AN EFFORT OVER AND OVER AGAIN. I TOLD MYSELF
AFTER THE NEXT AWAY TRIP, THE NEXT SERIES, THE
NEXT ALL-STAR WEEK, I'D REFOCUS. BUT I NEVER
DID, AND THERE AREN'T WORDS TO DESCRIBE HOW
SORRY I AM YOU HAD TO LEAVE FOR ME TO SEE WHAT
I WAS DOING. I'LL REGRET IT FOREVER.

I LOVE YOU.

Year Seven

His:

JESSIE BABY,

I'M SORRY I LED YOU ON WITH THE IDEA OF RETIRING. LOOKING BACK, IT FELT LIKE YOU WERE PUSHING FOR IT, BUT NOW I'M REALIZING IT WAS ALL ME. ALL IN MY HEAD. I USED THE IDEA OF RETIRING TO END THE FIGHT, BUT MY PLAYING BASEBALL WAS NEVER THE PROBLEM. THE PROBLEM WAS THE WAY I HAD MY HEAD UP MY ASS. YOU TOLD ME SO MANY TIMES WHAT YOU NEEDED, AND I SOMEHOW TRANSLATED IT INTO YOU WANTING ME TO RETIRE.

I'M ASHAMED OF HOW I PUSHED FOR A BABY THESE LAST FEW YEARS. YOU TOLD ME YOU DIDN'T WANT TO DO IT ALONE. I TOLD MYSELF YOU WOULDN'T BE ALONE WITH LEENA HERE AND THE FLASH WAGS. IT WAS NEVER ABOUT YOU BEING ALONE; IT WAS ABOUT YOU WANTING ME TO BE WITH YOU, NOT JUST PHYSICALLY

BUT MENTALLY. I'M SORRY I WASN'T THERE FOR YOU,
EVEN WHEN I WAS IN THE SAME ROOM.

I LOVE YOU.

Year Eight

His:

JESSIE BABY,

I WILL FOREVER BE ASHAMED THAT I WASN'T HONEST WITH YOU ABOUT HOW I FELT ABOUT RETIRING. AT THE MOMENT, IT MADE SENSE TO ME TO PROMISE YOU I WAS ALMOST DONE, LIKE THE FALSE PROMISE WOULD BE ENOUGH TO KEEP YOU HOLDING ON. I HATE HOW MISERABLE YOU WERE. I HATE HOW MY NEGLECT DID THIS TO YOU, TO US.

THE WORDS "I'M SORRY" ARE FEELING LIKE THEY'VE LOST THEIR MEANING, BUT I'LL SAY THEM TO YOU FOREVER IF YOU'LL LET ME.

I LOVE YOU.

Year Nine

His:

JESSIE BABY,

TO SAY READING THIS ENTRY WAS DEVASTATING IS AN UNDERSTATEMENT. YOU WERE HANGING BY A THREAD, AND I WAS IN MY OWN LITTLE WORLD. I WANT TO SAY I HAD EVERY INTENTION OF RETIRING THIS TIME, BUT I THINK WE BOTH KNOW IT'S NOT WHAT I WANTED. WHEN THE CALL CAME FROM COACH, I JUMPED AT IT. I FELT LIKE I HAD BEEN BOXED INTO A CORNER TO RETIRE, AND NOW I SEE IT WAS MY OWN DOING. BY NOT PAYING ATTENTION TO WHAT YOU REALLY NEEDED, I PUT US BOTH THROUGH HELL.

WHEN YOU FIRST WALKED AWAY, I WANTED TO CLING TO MY ANGER. HOW DARE SHE WALK AWAY? HOW DARE SHE NOT TELL ME SHE WAS UNHAPPY? BUT AFTER READING THIS JOURNAL, I CAN SEE JUST HOW HARD YOU TRIED. YOU TRIED FOR SO LONG, BABY,

AND I DON'T BLAME YOU AT ALL FOR LEAVING. IN FACT, I'M AMAZED YOU DIDN'T LEAVE ME SOONER. I FUCKING DESERVED IT. I DESERVE FOR YOU NEVER TO WANT TO SPEAK TO ME AGAIN.

I WILL FOREVER BE GRATEFUL FOR THESE LAST FEW MONTHS. YOU BEING WILLING TO EVEN CONSIDER GOING TO COUNSELING AND GIVING US A CHANCE TO WORK THINGS OUT WHEN I SPENT YEARS IGNORING YOUR NEEDS IS INCREDIBLE. YOU'RE INCREDIBLE, AND I WILL NEVER TAKE YOU FOR GRANTED AGAIN.

I LOVE YOU.

Year Ten

Hers:

His:

Jessie Baby,

US BEING STILL TOGETHER ENOUGH TO HIT THIS AN-
NIVERSARY IS NOTHING SHORT OF A MIRACLE. I'M
NOT SURE I'LL EVER UNDERSTAND HOW YOU COULD
HAVE BEEN WILLING TO GIVE ME THIS CHANCE. I WILL
NEVER STOP BEING GRATEFUL. KNOWING WHAT I
KNOW NOW, YOUR ABILITY TO EVEN CONSIDER FOR-
GIVING ME BLOWS MY MIND.

I KNOW BABY GIRL WAS A BIG FACTOR IN YOUR BEING WILLING TO EXPLORE THINGS, AND REALLY, IT JUST MAKES ME EVEN MORE THANKFUL. SHE'S SO LUCKY TO HAVE YOU AS A MOM, AND I WILL DO EVERYTHING IN MY POWER TO BE WORTHY OF BEING HER DAD.

I KNOW THE LAST TEN YEARS HAVE HAD MORE DOWNS THAN UPS, BUT I CAN ONLY PROMISE TO DO BETTER IF YOU GIVE ME THE CHANCE TO. I KNOW MY PROMISES DON'T HOLD MUCH WEIGHT, AND I KNOW I'VE MADE A WHOLE PILE OF MISTAKES OVER THE YEARS. THE ONLY THING I CAN DO IS BEG YOU TO GIVE ME THE CHANCE TO PROVE TO YOU THAT I SEE WHERE I WENT WRONG, AND I WILL NEVER MAKE THOSE SAME MISTAKES AGAIN. I'M SURE I'LL FIND NEW MISTAKES TO MAKE, BUT YOU WILL NEVER BE TAKEN FOR GRANTED. I WILL DO EVERYTHING I CAN TO PROVE IT TO YOU OVER AND OVER EVERY DAY FOR THE REST OF MY LIFE IF YOU'LL LET ME.

I LOVE YOU, JESSIE BABY. I'LL LOVE YOU UNTIL THE DAY I DIE, WHETHER WE'RE TOGETHER OR NOT.

Chapter Twenty-Two
Dan

I'VE BEEN WATCHING JESSIE carefully as I clean up dinner, and she reads through the journal. She looked freaked out when she realized I had read her entries, but thank God I did. The journal finally clued me in on everything she had been feeling. It's what woke me up and gave me a tiny chance at fixing things before it was too late. *Fuck.* I hope it's not too late.

Once I'm done cleaning everything up from dinner, I hover nearby. Glancing at her every time she turns a page. It's quiet in the yard; only the soft sounds of nature and Jessie's sniffling can be heard. I sneak closer to see that she's on the last entry. This is it. The moment of truth. Hopefully, now she'll have some insight into my mind like the girls suggested.

When she's done reading, she closes the journal and crumples in on herself, sobbing. I'm at her side in an instant, pulling her into my arms. The way she clings to me makes the small flicker of hope in my chest grow, like adding oxygen to a tiny flame.

"I'm so sorry, baby," I murmur into her hair. She pulls back from me and attempts to wipe her tears. When she turns her clear blue eyes my way, the look in them makes my chest squeeze and my breath hitch. She raises her hand and places it on my cheek. I want to close my eyes to contain my emotions, but I force myself to hold her gaze.

"I love you, Dan," she says so softly. I tense, waiting to see if she'll add a "but" to her sentence. Instead, she surprises me by saying with more confidence, "I want to come home."

I almost don't understand what she means. I'm afraid of letting my hopes get too high. "You want to come home?" I ask carefully.

She nods. "Yes. For good. I want to move back home. I want us to be together. Forever."

I blow out a huge breath as every tense muscle in my body relaxes, and tears start pouring down my face. I wanted to be all smooth and together for this, but the relief coursing through my body is turning me into a blubbering mess. I lower my head to her shoulder and cry as she holds me, chuckling softly.

"I think I've seen you cry more in the last six months than in the last thirteen years combined," she says lightly.

I huff out a laugh as I pull back to look at her. "Nothing has ever been as important to me as getting you back. Fixing the things I fucked up. Proving that I'm never going to take you for granted ever again." We stare into each other's eyes for a long moment before our mouths crash together.

If I thought the chemistry between us these last few months had been intense, it's nothing compared to this right here. I want to consume every part of her and bury myself so deep inside, she never stops feeling me. I want to mark her and claim her as mine, forever.

I pull her onto my lap and then stand, still holding her in my arms. She lets out a little squeal of surprise at the elevation change and wraps her legs around my waist, her baby bump pressed between us. I make a break for the house, and I only get as far as the kitchen island before I'm setting her down. I need to feel her, to taste her. The bedroom's too far away.

I don't waste any time before sliding up the short skirt of the dress she's wearing. I hook my fingers in the waistband of her silky underwear and slide them down her legs.

"Dan, please. I need you now. I can't wait," she pants out, desperately pulling on my belt and popping the button of my jeans.

"I can't wait either. I'll make it up to you next round," I say, dropping my jeans and underwear to the floor. I don't even bother stepping out of them before grabbing her hips to bring her to the edge of the countertop, the perfect height for me to take her standing. I slide home with little resistance thanks to how ready she is for me.

She lets out a soft moan as I bottom out before pulling almost all the way out, only to slam back in. Her hands roam, trying to grip the counter while her legs are locked around me. The heels of the boots she's still wearing are digging into my back as she attempts to pull me closer with every thrust.

"Oh God, please," she groans out, and I can feel how close she is. The walls of her pussy are squeezing and clenching around me, and I know I won't last much longer. I lean forward as much as I can without putting too much pressure on her belly. It's enough for me to pull one nipple into my mouth through the fabric of her dress. I thread a hand between us, and in the same moment I reach her clit, I bite down on her swollen nipple.

Jessie screams out a series of expletives mixed with my name as she explodes around me. I last another couple of thrusts before I'm following her over the edge and emptying myself inside of her with a groan. I rest for a moment with my head on her chest, and she plays with my hair as we both come down.

When I've caught my breath a bit, I shuffle to the bathroom, still wearing my shoes, my jeans, and briefs down around my ankles. Jessie giggles as she watches me go, so I don't bother trying to pull them up, gladly soaking up the sound of her laughter. Once I've cleaned us both up with a warm washcloth, I finally pull them up. She's moved to sit up on the counter, swinging her legs.

As I try to stand between her legs, I feel the small box still in its place in my pocket. This feels like as good a moment as any, so I back up to pull it out.

"I have something for you," I say, smiling at her. She eyes the box with eyebrows raised. I lean in, resting my arms on her thighs, still holding the box closed between us. "It comes with another apology. The girls mentioned you didn't like your engagement ring, so I—"

"I never said I didn't like it!" She pushes back on my shoulders to look me in the eye better. "Seriously, Dan, I loved it because it was from you."

"But it wasn't what you would have chosen," I say softly, no accusation in my tone. I can see it from the guilty look on her face; the girls were right. "Baby, it's okay. I'm not offended. But I needed to fix it."

I hold the box up again, but this time I pop the lid open, and she lets out a small gasp as she takes in the new ring. Instead of her plain solitaire diamond and simple wedding band set in yellow gold, the new ring set is a much more intricate design in shiny white gold. The center diamond is now surrounded by a square halo of smaller diamonds. An intricate infinity carving shines all the way around the bands. The jeweler was able to use her original yellow gold to fill in the carving, and the dual metallic tones shine beautifully.

"Oh, my God. It's so perfect. It's everything I would have picked myself." She sniffles a bit. "But what about my original ring? I don't want to just replace it with a new one."

I get a little nervous. I hope she approves of what I did, or we're gonna have the first fight of our renewed relationship.

"Well, this one is actually made with your original ring," I say cautiously. Her eyebrows shoot up, and she looks up at me, startled.

"What do you mean?" She gasps suddenly. "Did you steal my ring? I noticed it was missing, but I thought I had just not packed it when I moved!"

"Uh, well, technically Leena stole it."

She lets out a low chuckle as she shakes her head. I pull the ring out of the box to show it to her more closely.

"The jeweler who helped me with the design was able to work all the parts of your old ring into this one. The yellow gold along the bands is from your ring, and the center diamond is your original one. I thought about upgrading to a new, bigger one, but I didn't want to let go of the original." I take a deep breath before continuing. "Just like our relationship. We're not starting over from scratch. Everything we've been through in the last thirteen years will still be with us. Our first ten years of marriage aren't going to be erased. As much as I'd like to delete some parts of them, they'll always be with us. But hopefully, we can build something even more beautiful from here."

Tears slide down both of our faces, but the beaming smile on her face tells me these are happy ones. I know mine are.

"So, Jessie Baby, I'm asking you again. Will you marry me? I know we're still legally married, but I want us to do this right. I want to renew our vows. To have the wedding you really wanted back then. Maybe on our anniversary next year, so we can have our little flower girl there? What do you say? Will you re-marry me?"

She launches herself at me, throwing her arms around my neck, just like she did the first time I asked her all those years ago. She leans back and looks into my eyes. "Yes. My answer will always be yes. I love you."

"I love you too, Jessie Baby."

I slide the shiny new ring onto her finger and take what feels like my first full breath in months. Somehow, I got her back. She had every reason to walk away from me, from this, but she's choosing to forgive me. I know we'll still have our battles, and our time in couples counseling is far from over, but for now, I let myself feel the intense joy and relief that I got my girl back.

Both of my girls.

And I will never risk losing them ever again.

A few weeks later, we're at Songbird for our baby shower, which Annie and Leena insisted on rebranding as a "re-engagement party." It made Jessie laugh, so I just went with it. My mom is here permanently now. She moved up here last week for good, and it's already so nice having her as a part of our everyday life. We convinced her to stay with us, insisting we'll need all the help we can get once the baby comes.

She says she'll get her own place once we get the hang of things, but Jessie and I are hoping she'll move in permanently. We love the idea of our kids having their grandma just down a hallway, and I don't love the idea of her living alone as she gets older. She doesn't need our help now, but she may at some point. Either way, we'll cross that bridge when we get to it, and it's amazing not having her live states away.

I smile across the room as Jessie holds out her hand to show off her new ring. I shoot her a wink, and she sends me a beaming smile back. Bailey and Eric come up on either side of me and give me shit-eating grins.

"Glad you guys were able to work things out," Bailey says.

"Thanks, man. Me too. It was fucking close there for a minute," I blow out a breath. Just thinking about how close I came to losing Jessie makes my stomach clench, even weeks after Jessie moved back into the house.

"So what's your plan now that you're retired? You think you'll coach?" Eric asks. "Didn't the Flash have an opening?"

I shake my head. "Coach actually called and offered me a position, but I'm taking some time to focus on my family. I got my priorities fucked up before, and I'm not making the same mistake again. Maybe at some point, I'll get back into the baseball world, but I don't want to travel. I'm done being away from Jessie, especially with the baby coming."

Griffin comes up alongside Bailey as I'm talking. "I heard the high school here is gonna need a new baseball coach after this school year. Not a ton of travel with high school ball, right?"

"Huh, it could work. We'll see." I give the guys a smile and a couple of pats on the back before crossing the room to stand with my girls. Jessie smiles up at me as I reach out to run my hand over her quickly growing bump. At thirty weeks pregnant, she looks like she's smuggling a basketball under her pink floral dress.

"What did the guys want?" she murmurs as she tries to wrap her arms around my waist. Her arms almost can't reach with Baby Girl taking up the space between us.

"Eh, they were giving me ideas for new jobs. Apparently, the high school will need a new baseball coach next year."

"Is it something you want to do?" she asks carefully.

I shrug. "Could be fun, but right now I'm rather enjoying my time off." I kiss my way down her neck before grabbing her hand and pulling her back behind the bar and into the back kitchen area. I move her around the corner a bit, out of sight of anyone who comes in for glassware or garnishes.

"What are you doing?" she whispers.

"Just wanted some privacy to make out with my wife," I whisper back into her ear. She lets out a low chuckle that goes straight to my cock. I back Jessie up against a counter, kissing her soundly. As I reach for the hem of her dress, we're joined by two angry, whispering voices entering the kitchen.

"Are we ever going to talk about it?"

"There's nothing to fucking talk about."

"I can't stop thinking about you... about that night."

"It was one night. You have to let it go."

"Spitfire, please."

"Don't call me that!"

"Tell me you don't feel this pull. Tell me you don't want me as badly as I want you. Tell me you're not soaking wet for me right now, and I'll drop it."

There's a long, heated silence. Jessie and I stare at each other with wide eyes, taking in the conversation we are clearly not meant to be hearing. We can't see them, but Cass and Griffin's voices are unmistakable.

Finally, Cass speaks again. "None of it matters. I don't do relationships, Griffin. I don't do complications. And you, Mr. My-boss-slash-best-friend's-fiancée's-brother-with-two-kids-and-an-ex-wife, are a walking complication. I'm sorry."

We hear Cass walk away, and I sneak a glance around the corner to see Griffin run both hands down his face, adjust himself in his jeans, and follow her out.

"Holy shit!" Jessie whispers. "What the hell? I knew something was happening with them."

"They did act fucking weird the first night Griffin was here. Do you think they hooked up before? He didn't say anything about it when he was helping me at the house."

"I don't know, but now I'm dying to find out."

I'm about to pick up where we left off, but we hear Leena's voice echo close to the door, "Has anyone seen Jessie? Or Dan? Did they sneak upstairs, those horny fucks?"

We both burst out laughing. "Upstairs probably would have been a better plan," I murmur, adjusting myself in my pants as Jessie fixes her lipstick.

"I think Cass was moving in there for a while. Plus, we wouldn't have overheard the drama." She waggles her eyebrows at me, making me laugh again.

"I love you."

"I love you, too. You ready for our duet?" She smirks, knowing I'm nervous because she picked a fucking fast song, but at this point, I know I'd do anything for this woman. Especially after having her home these last few weeks and getting a front-row seat to exactly how uncomfortable she is. I can't even imagine how much worse it's going to get over the next ten or so weeks, so I'd go along with pretty much anything to make her smile.

Which is why ten minutes later, I'm on the Songbird stage singing "Crazier Than You" from *The Addams Family* musical with the very pregnant love of my life. She's laughing because she keeps having to gasp for air with how fast the song is and how much the baby is pressing up into her ribs.

The bar is filled with our friends and family, all smiling and laughing with us as we sing this ridiculous song. I let my gaze travel over all the people I love, finally landing on the one I love most, and I'm hit with a wave of emotion. I could have missed this.

We could have been estranged, on our way to divorce, and planning to pass our baby back and forth if I hadn't come to my senses and fought for us. Feeling all the love brimming in this room, one thing I know for sure is I won't ever risk this again.

I thought playing pro baseball was living the life of my dreams. Don't get me wrong, my career was incredible, and I'm grateful I got the privilege of having the type of dream job only a few achieve. But this right here? This is the life of my dreams, and I will never take it for granted again.

The party goes late, way longer than a normal baby shower would go. Jessie is snuggled up against me on one of the comfy couches. As we sit and chat with our chosen family late into the evening, our eyes meet, and I do my best to memorize this moment in time.

There isn't anywhere else I'd rather be.

Epilogue
Jessie

Two Months Later

A soft knock on the door wakes me out of the fitful sleep I was in, and I immediately look around the hospital room for the baby. I find her snuggled in her daddy's arms as he smiles down at her, a look of pure adoration on his face.

Charlotte Marlene Chase was born yesterday evening, two days after her due date. We kept waiting for me to go into labor, and when my due date came and went, Dr. Sharon ordered an ultrasound to check everything out. Turns out little Lottie never moved into the head-down position, even though three different doctors in my practice told me she was over the last few weeks. Apparently, during all of their wildly uncomfortable checks each week, they were feeling her bottom instead of her head.

A few hours later, we were at the hospital ready to have a C-section and get our little girl out of there. I didn't have any strong feelings either way about our birth plan, and if I'm being totally honest, I was glad not to have to do the whole labor part. Of course, the searing pain across my stomach and my complete inability to use my ab muscles have made me sure this was not in any shape or form the easy way out.

No matter how she entered this world, she's perfect, and I'm just so happy she's here. I always loved her, but I was still unprepared for just how intensely the love grew when I got to meet her face-to-face. I was even more unprepared for how it would feel to witness Dan becoming a dad. If I hadn't already fallen deeper in love with him over the last few months, this would have done it.

The song "Everything Changes" from *Waitress,* the musical, keeps popping into my mind. The line is something like, "we were both born today," and it's exactly how I feel. I'm a whole new person now that I'm Lottie's mom.

The knock that woke me up turns out to be Leena and Annie coming in to visit their niece. Bailey and Eric follow them in, weighed down by balloons, flowers, and a giant stuffed teddy bear that I will scold someone for when I'm less blissed out.

Leena walks straight to me, bending to give me a careful hug. "How you doing, mama?"

"Good. I mean, it hurts to laugh, or cough, or move, but she is so fucking worth it."

Dan lets out a low chuckle as he hands Lottie to Leena, and Annie takes her place at my side.

"She's so precious, Jess. You did so good."

I grin up at her. All three of our guys are smiling down at Leena, holding the little blanket-wrapped bundle containing my daughter, and I'm overcome with joy. Eventually, they all take turns holding her, marveling at her little coos and stretches.

When she fusses, she's passed back to me to try nursing. We seem to be getting the hang of it now, but shit, it hurts when she latches on. Hopefully, it goes away as we get used to breastfeeding, because ouch.

Once the pain subsides, I watch her little face for a moment before refocusing on the people in the room. "Alright," I say as if I'm calling a meeting to order. "Who's having one next? Lottie needs friends."

I stare up at my two best friends and almost immediately Annie's finger flies to her nose to show she's "not it." We all laugh, and Eric kisses the side of her head as he rolls his eyes. They're not even engaged yet, so I'm not really surprised by her antics.

Leena and Bailey share a soft smile and a nod before she clears her throat. "Actually, I'm up next."

My jaw drops as happy tears fill my eyes. I was mostly messing with them and didn't expect this wonderful news. "Oh, Leena, I'm so happy for you. For you both!"

"Thanks, babes. It's still early days. We just found out last week, so anything could still happen, but we're excited." She shoots me a timid smile, and Annie wraps her in a big hug. Dan and Eric take turns giving Bailey bro hugs and patting him on the back.

I sit and watch my favorite people in the world chatter and smile, filled with such overwhelming joy. I can see it already. Our beautiful backyard, filled with our chosen family. The kids all running around and playing together. Growing up more like cousins than friends. The complete opposite of the cold, lonely childhood I had.

This year may have been fucking intense and so difficult, but it makes this moment even sweeter. In February, the life of my dreams seemed so far out of reach, I almost gave up all hope. But here we are in November, and I literally could not be happier.

Sometimes you have to walk away to find out exactly what is meant for you. The love you're meant to have will follow. The people who are supposed to be in your life will fight for you. I will never stop being grateful that Dan didn't give up. Our marriage may have had a little meltdown, but we've built it back so much stronger.

Strong enough to last forever.

The End

Thank you for reading The Marriage Meltdown! Want more Dan & Jessie? Scan here for a free bonus epilogue!

Curious about any of the music found in *The Marriage Meltdown*? Checkout this playlist to find all of the songs mentioned as well as a few extras!

Next Up

Cass and Griffin's age gap, single-dad story is next in The Chemistry Complication.

See Where it Started

Turn the page to go back to the beginning with Leena & Bailey's story in The Songbird Setup.

The Songbird Setup

Leena

"I LOVE TO SING sad songs. For anyone who doesn't know me: I'm Leena, the owner of the Songbird Cafe and Bar. For those who are already familiar, this is old news, but for anyone new to our open mic night, I like to kick things off with this disclaimer." I laugh softly into the microphone.

The crowd chuckles, and some shake their heads, but they humor me. They know that if I perform at my cafe's open mic night, nine times out of ten, I will choose a slow, sad ballad.

Some of the most interesting songs to sing happen to be slow, heart-wrenching melodies, and I've always gravitated towards them. This is why going to karaoke nights with friends causes problems for me. Karaoke has this fun, crazy vibe, and nothing can kill the vibe faster than belting about lost love or singing a mournful song about heartbreak.

"My love of sad songs is exactly why, when I opened Songbird, I started open mic nights. I was tired of feeling left out at karaoke and just wanted to sing what I wanted to sing." I go on to detail the rules of our open mic nights.

"Rule #1: We do not tolerate heckling or booing of any kind. This is a safe space for anyone to perform whatever they want. Art is subjective. If you don't like someone's performance, use that time to visit the bar or the bathroom. It's the in-person equivalent of 'just keep scrolling.' Leave the mean comments for your social media feeds." I give the crowd a quick, serious-faced stare to make certain they understand that even though I'm cracking jokes, I'm dead serious about the rules, and in case there is anyone who thinks I'm kidding, I go on.

"Rule #2: We reserve the right to boot your ass if you break rule #1." I raise my eyebrows and make eye contact with a table of twenty-something guys that I haven't seen before. They nod their understanding and a couple of them hold up their hands in an expression of innocence, letting me know that they'll behave.

"Finally, rule #3: Have fun. This isn't life or death. Everyone will move on with their lives, whether you give the performance of a lifetime or completely forget every line of your new slam poem." I smile and the crowd chuckles. I sit down at the keyboard and lower the mic with me. "My final warning is that we do a lot of Broadway numbers here, and while you're welcome to do whatever you like for your turn—I'll never turn down anyone who wants to cover some Taylor Swift classics—show tunes are my jam and I play what I want!" I shrug my shoulders as I play the intro for "Burn" from *Hamilton*. Someone near the back whoops and I laugh into the microphone.

"Sounds like we've got some Lin-Manuel Miranda fans in the back," I sweep my gaze around the room, "Or maybe this is just the 'I've been cheated on and it sucks' anthem."

The laughter of the crowd gives me the same rush it always does. Laughter and applause are the best medicine and performing always helps me to become lighter and less haunted. I give myself over to that emotion as I launch into the song, wishing I could feel this free all the time rather than my default settings of melancholy and sarcastic.

The lift performing gives me is one of the main reasons that I often open and close the open mic night lineup. I like to give my speech about the rules and what to expect. I also like to say goodnight to the loyal customers who drank with us all night. Plus, I have very little social life, so the twice-a-week open mic nights get me out of my small apartment above the cafe and out of my head for a little while.

The Songbird Cafe and Bar is a large open rectangular room. The bar runs along the right side of the room with open back barstools along the front. Seating is a mix of cozy chairs and couches, with high-top tables scattered throughout the room. I wanted to create a place for anyone to hang out, no matter the time of day. We even have a few racks of donated new and used books that operate like a little free library along the left side of the room, for anyone looking for something to read while they relax in our comfy vibe.

Towards the back of the bar, we have a barista station that handles all the morning cafe drinks with a pastry case that we fill from local bakeries. A mirrored wall displays an assortment of liquor and mixers, and we offer a selection of local beers on tap for our evening crowd. Most people will bring takeout since we don't have a full kitchen.

The stage, complete with microphone, electric keyboard, and speaker system, sits in the left corner for our open mic nights. I bought a gently used karaoke setup from a bar that was going out of business to add options for open mic nights.

I started open mic nights about two months after opening Songbird. Morning coffee and pastry sales were good, but I wanted a reason for people to come out in the evening. I had the idea one weekend after some friends dragged me out for karaoke and I couldn't sing what I wanted without bringing down the entire room. In the year since, they've become increasingly popular and we always have a full crowd.

As I come to the end of "Burn," I let myself get a little lost in the lyrics and the thoughts of the past bubble up. It's been two years since my life blew up, but somehow the wounds are still fresh when I'm performing like this. However, there is something cathartic—like I'm working through some of the damage—when I get lost in the song lyrics.

After playing the final notes, the crowd applauds, and whoops and my spirit lifts. I take just a second to enjoy the moment and then I put the past back in the box in the back of my mind where it belongs.

"Thank you, everyone!" I say, hoping the sincerity in my voice is perceived by the crowd. "Next up we've got Stella and Ian to entertain us with their acoustic stylings." The singer-songwriter duo that's always popular with the crowd takes the stage and gets set up with their acoustic guitars. They start with a really cool cover of *NSYNC's "Bye Bye Bye" before launching into some of their original pieces. I hang out at the bar to listen for a little while and then continue on with my Tuesday night.

Later that week, I'm helping Cass tend the bar before the start of open mic. For a Friday night in early January, we're super busy. We've had an unseasonably warm week and more people are here without the snow and ice encouraging them to stay home. On top of that, we're short-handed tonight since our weekend bartender, Alaina, is out with the flu.

Cass is Songbird's full-time general manager and has been with me from the start. She is a total rock star when it comes to running the business side. We met in my junior year of college when she was a freshman. Cass and I hit it off right away back then, and she's become one of my best friends now that we're running Songbird together.

We reconnected after Cass finished her MBA from Ohio State. After she graduated, I asked if she wanted to help me open my own place. She grew up working in her family's restaurant in West Virginia and it gave her the perfect experience for running a cafe and bar. I prefer to focus more on the creative side of the business like fun events and the ambiance of the space.

Cass and I have only gotten closer during the year she's worked for me. Our personalities mesh perfectly and there's no one else I would want running my business. We're both snarky and fluent in sarcasm and inappropriate jokes. We like to joke that we are twins separated at birth, although we look nothing alike.

In appearance, we're total opposites, with her tall willowy frame and dark straight hair that is cut into a short, smooth bob framing her face perfectly. I'm several inches shorter with curves for days. I usually pull my unruly auburn curls up into a bun or Dutch braid to keep them out of my way.

"What depressing ballad are you kicking off open mic with tonight?" Cass murmurs with a smirk. She is not a fan of my penchant for sad songs and likes to remind me of that fact often. If Cass gets up to sing, she usually goes with something fun and upbeat—she has no problems fitting in at karaoke—although she loves show tunes as much as I do.

"I'm thinking it's a Sara Bareilles sort of night," I smirk as she rolls her eyes and sighs.

"Whatever floats your boat, boss-lady!"

"Thank you so much for your support." I snark back at her and laugh as I stroll up to the piano. I sit down and sigh, with tiredness weighing on my body.

A recurring nightmare featuring my asshole of an ex made for a night of shitty sleep. I woke up in a pool of sweat with my heart pounding. It took me a while to shake off the panic and rush of adrenaline. I had a hard time sleeping after that so I'm exhausted, emotionally drained, and downcast today. Sara Bareilles's songs are like my performance security blanket, always there when I need to let the emotions flow.

I run through my usual welcome speech with the rules of open mic night and start playing "Gravity" which is one of my absolute favorites. This song has carried me through several heartbreaks and always feels relevant. I hear the door open as I start the second verse, but I don't bother looking up. People come and go a lot through open mic night and I prefer to let myself get lost in the lyrics.

As I come to the bridge, a chill runs up my spine, and I can sense someone watching from near the door. We dim the lights in the bar so I can't see him very well, only his very tall frame standing watching me sing.

The hairs on my arm stand on end and my heart rate picks up. It reminds me a little of the adrenaline I experienced after my nightmare, but this time I'm not scared. I'm intrigued. I have never in my life been so aware of someone's physical presence in my life and I silently hope the tall stranger will stick around so I can figure out why. Maybe I know him?

After I finish my number and hand off the mic to the next act, I pop behind the bar to help Cass manage the crowd that has built up. I'm so focused on running drinks that when I look up and find the mystery man sitting at the bar in front of me, I'm almost startled. Not just because of the reaction my body seems to have to his presence, but also because he is stunning.

His dark wavy hair is close-cropped on the sides and worn a little longer on top. He has the perfect amount of scruff covering his chiseled jaw, somewhere between a five o'clock shadow and a full beard. His dark brown eyes have a spark of humor in them and follow me as I approach. Even sitting on the bar stool, I have to look up at him to get his order.

"Hi there! What can I get you?" I chirp, trying not to let on how his presence is affecting me. If he knew me at all, he'd see right through me. Most of my regulars are used to me being grumpy or snarky with them. I rarely do the upbeat customer service voice but something about him makes me nervous.

He takes a glance at our beer list. "I'll take the Wolf's Ridge lager on tap, thanks," he answers with a smooth, deep voice and a smile.

"Be right back with that!" I take off to pour his drink at the other end of the bar with my hands shaking.

What the hell is wrong with me? He hasn't even said anything real, just ordered a beer, but my heart is beating like he asked me to marry him.

Whoa.. marry him? Where the actual fuck did that thought come from? I berate myself as I pour his beer. I'm not sure I believe in marriage anymore. I'm certainly not in the habit of imagining strangers proposing to me.

As soon as the thought crosses my mind, I picture it. This beautiful man, down on one knee, holding my hand and looking up at me in adoration. It's enough to make my stomach churn and I'm even more nervous as I head back towards him. I set the glass on a coaster in front of him as he slides a twenty across the bar.

"I'll just be right back with your change!" I slowly slide away as I'm talking. I want to both be near him and get as far away as possible at the same time, and it's scrambling my brain a bit.

"Nah, keep the change. " He gives me a small smile and my stomach bottoms out while my heart rate climbs.

"Oh! Thank you!" I give him a genuine smile despite my unease. Cass is saving up for a down payment on a new car and generous tippers are always welcome at my bar. I glance around for the next customer when I realize the line is slowing down and everyone has been helped. I start to walk away when the handsome stranger stops me.

"Wait! I ... uh ... I actually came over here to talk to you," he says in a rush. I raise my eyebrows at that and wait for him to elaborate. "I was walking past and heard you singing and I just had to find out where that voice was coming from." He finishes quickly, seeming mildly embarrassed by the confession.

"Well, I'll be damned," I quip. "I guess I owe some cartoon fairytale writers an apology!" The snarky comment makes me feel a little more like myself. My cheeks are blushing from his compliment, but I can't keep the sarcasm from flying out of my mouth.

"What do you mean?" He asks and I laugh while rolling my eyes before launching into one of my favorite tirades.

"Fairy tales completely set me up for disappointment when all the boys growing up didn't give two shits about my singing voice." I realize I'm about to confess an old insecurity, but I'm not able to stop myself. "For a chubby, awkward teenager who was way too into musical theater, the promise that my prince charming just needed to hear me sing to be interested definitely did not pan out the way I hoped." I laugh and only just barely keep the bitterness out of my voice.

The gorgeous stranger chuckles kindly and takes a slow up-and-down glance at my body that sets my skin tingling. After years of work on my self-esteem, I love—or at least feel some neutrality about—my mid-size curvy body. I no longer beat myself up about my pant size having double digits and I refuse to even own a scale.

But in the gaze of this stunning man, I'm feeling self-conscious. What is he seeing when he looks at me? I think I'm detecting a hint of heat in his eyes, and that makes me blush all over again. I'm sure he notices my cheeks burning but is nice enough not to mention it.

"Do you think your manager would mind if I bought you a drink?" He asks with a smile. He clearly missed the part of my welcome speech where I mentioned that I'm the owner of the bar. So I play along and pour myself a gin and Sprite.

"I don't think she would mind at all," I smirk as I sip the drink. He's just about to say something when the alarm on my phone goes off, making me jump. I look down at my watch to see that it's almost nine and time for my weekly FaceTime with Annie.

My two best friends and I have been a tight-knit trio since we met in the seventh grade. For years, it was Annie, Jessie, and me. We did everything together, all the way through college at Ohio State, before going our separate ways.

Jessie and I have found our way back to Fort Starling, but Annie moved to Chicago a few years ago and her job keeps her crazy busy. We've taken to scheduling our FaceTimes to make sure we stay in touch. I miss her big time, so I am not in the habit of bailing on our calls, but the handsome guy in front of me makes it tempting.

"Oh shit, I have a phone call I have to take!" I say apologetically.

That I even for a second considered blowing off Annie for this guy makes my stomach drop. What am I even doing? I'm not interested in dating anyone. I don't want a relationship. What is even the point of staying here chatting with him when I'm not interested in it going any further than a drink in my bar? He nods like he isn't sure whether I'm telling the truth or blowing him off, and for some reason, I can't stop myself from continuing our exchange.

"Will you be around for a while? I'll be back down to close out open mic at midnight." I hear the pleading tone in my voice that low-key embarrasses me, but can't quite make it stop. He checks his phone and shrugs a bit.

"I've got kind of an early morning, so I'm not sure if I can stick around," he says regretfully.

"Oh okay. Well... it was really nice to meet you!" I say too loudly and spin around. I take off through the door to the kitchen so he doesn't see the disappointment and confusion blazing across my face.

It's only as I'm climbing the stairs to my apartment over the bar that I realize we didn't even exchange names. He's still a mystery and that's probably for the best. I actually hope he's not there when I go back down to the bar. For the most part, I believe my own lies.

Scan here to continue reading!

Acknowledgements

I can't believe we're here at the end of my third book! I heard somewhere that it takes around three books to really be considered established as an author so I guess this means I'm official now. I'm so lucky to have found something I love to do as much as writing down the stories that live in my brain!

Writing is a wildly solitary thing but authoring isn't and I couldn't do it without some amazing people!

First up, as always, is my wonderfully supportive husband for always cheering on my authoring. I'm sorry I made some strangers on Threads think I was divorcing you but in my defense, anyone that thought that, just didn't read to the end! Marketing's gotta do what marketing's gotta do!

To my kiddos, thank you for tolerating me writing at all hours and being incredibly invested in my TikTok making process.

Huge shout out to the author friends in the Nighttime Sprinters chat. You all have been so instrumental in teaching me so much about the indie author world and making this career feel a little less lonely!

Thank you Keri for inspiring Jessie's need to sniff alcoholic drinks while pregnant!

Thank you to my editor Lily Luchesi from Partners In Crime Book Services! I swear I've learned my lesson and will avoid the word "that" for the rest of my author career.

A huge thank you to my beta readers: Kaitlin, Katie, Abby, Mave, Cori, and Shelby! Your feedback was so helpful in polishing Dan and Jessie's story. I love reading all of your comments and reactions!

As always, a shout out to my forever faves Taco Bell and BIGGBY Coffee!

Last but certainly not least thank you to the readers that take a chance on indie authors with tiny followings. Every purchase and page read means the world to me! Love you, book besties!

xo, *Maggie*

Also by Maggie

The Songbird Cafe Series

The Songbird Setup (Leena & Bailey)

The Boss Boycott (Annie & Eric)

The Marriage Meltdown (Jessie & Dan)

The Chemistry Complication (Cass & Griffin)

About the Author

MAGGIE LINN SHARPE HAS been creating worlds and characters in her mind for as long as she can remember. Because no career path felt quite right, despite her efforts, and motherhood limited her social time, she decided to try writing a romance novel. Now she's pretty sure she won't be able to stop.

Maggie lives outside of Columbus, Ohio with her husband, her two boys, and her mother. When she's not writing, she's usually reading romance, obsessing about musicals, or spending time with her kiddos, which usually involves learning more than she wanted to know about Minecraft and watching Bluey on repeat.□

Connect with Maggie

www.ingramcontent.com/pod-product-compliance
Lightning Source LLC
Chambersburg PA
CBHW050036120726
47903CB00006B/2060